Code Name: Viking is a novel based on actual events that took place in Europe in the mid 1960's. It is not meant to be a historical or chronological record of events. Some characters are based on actual persons, however, names, nationalities and locations may have been changed to shield there actual identities. There is no malicious intent by the author to discredit or malign any person or group of persons. There are certain events in the book that are based on speculation and others that I will neither confirm or deny.

An original novel by:

Ronald E. Whitley

With a special thanks to:

Kevin Lamar Allmon, Continuity Reader

Read also:

The Pacific Hotel, by Ronald E. Whitley, Trafford Publishing, ISBN 1-4120-9462-3 Available at trafford.com/06-1217

Author welcomes questions and comments and may be contacted at PO Box 424, Brandenburg, KY, USA, 40108

Order this book online at www.trafford.com/07-1397
or email orders@trafford.com

Most Trafford titles are also available at major online book retailers.

Note for Librarians: A cataloguing record for this book is available from Library and Archives Canada at www.collectionscanada.ca/amicus/index-e.html

Printed in Victoria, BC, Canada.

ISBN: 978-1-4251-3577-5

We at Trafford believe that it is the responsibility of us all, as both individuals and corporations, to make choices that are environmentally and socially sound. You, in turn, are supporting this responsible conduct each time you purchase a Trafford book, or make use of our publishing services. To find out how you are helping, please visit www.trafford.com/responsiblepublishing.html

Our mission is to efficiently provide the world's finest, most comprehensive book publishing service, enabling every author to experience success. To find out how to publish your book, your way, and have it available worldwide, visit us online at www.trafford.com/10510

 www.trafford.com

North America & international
toll-free: 1 888 232 4444 (USA & Canada)
phone: 250 383 6864 • fax: 250 383 6804 • email: info@trafford.com

The United Kingdom & Europe
phone: +44 (0)1865 722 113 • local rate: 0845 230 9601
facsimile: +44 (0)1865 722 868 • email: info.uk@trafford.com

10 9 8 7 6 5 4 3 2 1

Code Name: VIKING

by

Ronald E. Whitley

INTRODUCTION

The Bay of Pigs, the Cuban Missile Crisis, JFK sending advisors to Vietnam and Bobby hounding Jimmy Hoffa and chasing the mob. Events shortly followed by the assassination in Dallas, are all recent events just prior to my joining the Army. The Cold War is in full bloom and everyone is spying on everyone else, even allies spy on allies. No one trusts anyone and no agency shares information with any other agency, unless it is to their advantage. Mistrust and suspicion are the order of the day and the state of international affairs.

So follow this story of a young soldier, as circumstances beyond his control, pull him into the dark, dangerous, deceitful world of spies, lies, drugs and murder. A world where at times it is impossible to distinguish between the good guys and the bad guys. A world where black and white, good and evil only depend on your personal point of view, and even then, they are not so far apart. A world where some men betray their countries for money, sex, drugs or to conceal some perverted secret, while others betray their countries because they are true believers. There are, indeed, true believers on all sides. Men and women willing to do what ever it takes or even give their lives for an idea or belief. Then there are the freelancers and professionals who make a living out of all the paranoia running loose in the world. Liars, cheats, blackmailers and thieves, all of them, whose only God is money.

I dedicate this book to the memory of John Fallon Roark, one of our true believers, who gave his life in South America in 1984, and all the true believers like him, who are now just stars on a wall.

CHAPTER 1.

In The Beginning

A troop ship crossing the Atlantic destination Germany, 1966

I think back to that first day, on a bus headed to Fort Knox, how scared I was, feeling shaky inside, wondering what I had gotten myself into by joining the Army. Just a young kid off on an unknown adventure to start my life, little did I know, just how far that bus would take me.

The racks on this old tub are six high in our compartment, if you can call it that, there are eighteen of us in this small room, about as far forward and as far down as they put troops on this ship. The General Patch, some how the name fits this rusted old bucket. This was the last trip for the General Patch, there was over two thousand of us on the way to Germany, then a load back to the States and then on to that big ocean in the sky, or what ever it is that happens to these old rust buckets, more likely to a scrap yard some where on the east coast.

We are in cabin D, section one, deck four, and our mess, is in section two, deck two. We had maps, but it still took a couple of times of getting lost, and the first few times we arrived about the time our half hour for meals was up, just enough time to grab some fruit off the line. Everyone didn't go up for meals the first day or two, a lot of the guys were sea sick, but not me. I took every opportunity to get out of our room, it was hot crowded and stunk like a high school football locker room after a big game. Our section was allowed on the forward deck four hours a day, but it didn't take long to learn the ends and outs, and I started sneaking up to the deck during section two's time and in the evenings.

There were two cabins on deck four, that were never called on for work details, ours and the one next to us. I don't think they normally housed troops in these two rooms, and no one bothered to change the ships work assignment schedule. A few times when I snuck up to the deck, it was during a sweep down, so I would just grab a broom and join in, but after I learned the schedule by heart, I would arrive just after the work was over.

Five and a half days and we are entering the English Channel and it is rough, almost everyone was getting sick, it sure was different from steaming across the Atlantic, it seemed like we weren't going anywhere, just bobbing up and down, and rocking back and forth. The heads are all stopped up by this time and full of puck and excrement, the only hope of getting away from the foul smell and stale air in the cabin was the deck and none of the troops were allowed on deck when it was raining, and it has been doing nothing but raining since we entered the channel.

A day and a half later and we finally entered the Port of Bremerhaven and in another five or six hours we will be off this tub.

I had my orders, I was being assigned to the

American Embassy in Bonn, and I had no idea what I was going to be doing there. I went to basic training at Fort Knox, then eight weeks in demolition school learning how to blow things up. I did so well in school that after graduation, they sent me to Fort Lenordwood to another eight weeks of engineer explosives, and I thought I finally had my calling, then came my first real assignment. I was assigned to Fort Sill, Oklahoma and ended up as a clerk in a 105 Howitzer Battery in the 2d of the 2d Field Artillery. The Old Duce, that is what they called it, but Old Duce was actually the name of the battalion mascot, a mule that lived better than we did. He had his private barn and his own personal G I to take care of him. That's the Army for you, all that training, and now I have to learn how to blow up a typewriter. I was having such a hard time struggling with trying to type morning reports and training schedules, that the Battery Commander, Captain Johnston and the First Sergeant took pity on me and sent me to a typing class on post. The instructor that taught the class at the Education Center took an interest in me because I picked up typing so fast and enrolled me in the GED program to take classes at night. After I got my GED they gave me some college level equivalency exams. I passed five of the six test they gave me, got some college credit under my belt and started taking correspondence courses and classes at the Education Center at night offered by the University of Maryland.

So while the other GIs were out drinking and having a good old time, I spent my free time studying and evenings taking college classes at the Ed Center. I grew up a lot in my first year and a half in the army,

I went from being a scared know nothing high school drop out to a hell of a clerk with an Associates Degree in Business Administration and could not only burn up my typewriter, but blow it up as well.

One day I got a call from the Battalion Personnel Officer saying he wanted to see me. I figured I was going to get reassigned to Battalion, but I was wrong. He told me that I had an appointment to see a Major at Forth Army Headquarters for an interview. The next day I went to the interview, but it was strange, it seemed more like an inquisition than a interview for a job. He asked me a lot of personal questions about my family, did I have a girl friend, why I had dropped out of high school, and why I spent so much time at the Ed Center, then he gave me an Army Manual and told me to read the first two chapters. I did, then he took the book back and told me to recite back to him what I read. I must not have done very well with the interview, because he told me I could go back to my unit, and that was the end of it.

The First Sergeant out of the clear blue put me in for promotion and I did well at the promotion board and got to take off my mosquito wings and sew on the eagles of a brand new Specialist Four. Two weeks later I came down on the overseas levy, got my orders and here I am about to start a new adventure in Germany.

It seemed like hours, but we finally got off the General Patch and went to a reception center where they fed us and started some processing. Most of the other guys just had orders to United States Army, Europe, and had to wait for unit assignments, but some of us already had assignments, so that night, I was put on a train to Frankfurt with instructions to report in at the transportation office at the train station when I got there.

It was late when we pulled in and the Sergeant in charge took the eight of us arriving on the train, to the 5th Corps reception station to spend the night. The next morning after breakfast another Sergeant picked us up and took us back to the train station, all but three of us that is, the other three had assignments in the Frankfurt area and stayed at the reception station.

Back at the station, I was given a train ticket to Bonn and told to check in with the Military Information Officer when I got there. Germany is beautiful and I was excited and could hardly wait to get to my new job, get settled in so I could get out and explore this new and wonderful place. I say new, new to me anyway, everything looked so old and historic and full of new things to see and experience. It was a combination of old world and new modern buildings mixed together. Clean streets and streetcars set in the middle of old medieval looking statues and architecture, it would be like being able to go back in time and take a walk through history. I knew I was going to love it here.

When I arrived in Bonn the British Sergeant at the Information Booth made a phone call for me and told me to have a seat and someone would come to pick me up. In about twenty minutes a Marine Staff Sergeant, wearing dress blue paints and a tan uniform shirt, showed up and asked if I was the new guy, looked at my orders, then told me to grab my duffle and follow him.

"I'm Staff Sergeant Posey. What's your name again, WHITELY?"

"No Sergeant, it's Whitley."

"OK, Whitley, throw your gear in the rear." He said as he motioned to the jeep parked next to the curb at the side entrance of the train station.

It was a short, five minute ride to the Embassy and Sergeant Posey blew the horn as we approached the vehicle gate. The gate opened and another Marine waved us in, as we drove around to the back of the classical looking building. Sergeant Posey pulled up to the back door of the south wing and stopped but didn't turn the engine off.

"This is it, grab your bag, through the door, down the stairs, end of the hallway last office on the left."

I had no sooner got my duffle out of the back of the jeep when Sergeant Posey pulled away and headed on down the ornately landscaped drive. I followed his directions and went into the building and down the stairs. I briefly looked at the information board on the wall at the bottom of the stairs, then continued on down the hall.

The sign on the outside of the door read, ASST. MILITARY ATTACH'E. I knocked on the door but there was no answer, so I knocked louder, still no answer, so I tried the doorknob, it was unlocked but before I could open it, I was startled by a voice behind me.

"Are you looking for me?"

I turned around to see a, fit looking guy in civilian clothes, with short cropped military style hair, I figured he was in his early thirties. "Yes Sir, I think so, I was told to report to the last office on the left."

"I'm Master Sergeant Peacoe, who the hell are

you?"

"Specialist Whitley, Sir, I'm being assigned here."

"The hell you say. Well, what are you waiting for, go on in and have a seat and let me see your orders."

"Yes Sir." I said as I opened the door and held it open for him.

"The first thing is, you can drop that *Sir* shit. Sit down and let me see your orders." He said as he sat the cup of coffee he was carrying down and took a seat behind the big oak desk that was scattered with papers.

I sat my duffle bag down and took a seat in the chair beside his desk and handed him the large sealed envelope with several copies of my orders stapled to it.

He opened the envelope and took out my 201 file and started to read it then pulled a copy of my orders off the front and stared at them for a moment than back to the 201 file. "You didn't go to the Defense Language School at the Presidio, where did you learn your German?" He asked without looking up from the file.

"I don't speak German, Sir, I mean Sergeant."

He glanced up and looked at me and asked. "Russian?"

"No, Sergeant."

"What the hell languages do you speak?"

"Just English, Sergeant."

"Well this doesn't make any since, first of all we don't have a slot for a Spec 4, the only position we have open right now is for a Spec 6 Attaché Specialist, but you're not even close to being eligible for promotion and second, you don't speak German, and third, you don't even have a security clearance. What the hell am I suppose to do with you?"

"I don't know Sergeant."

"You don't know much of anything, do you soldier? Well, I'll tell you this, Major Bestler isn't going to like this shit, at all. You just stay here for a little while and I'll be back. Smoke if you want to and there is a room with some vending machines, back down the hall on the left next to the head."

"Yes, Sergeant." I said as he got up and took my files and left the room. I got up and walked to the latrine then thought I'd get a soda out of one of the machines in the vending room. There was a couple of young guys, about my age or a little older, sitting at a table talking, but when I walked into the room they stopped and just looked at me. I figured they were Marines by their haircuts, they didn't say anything to me, just kind of nodded then continued talking when I left the room.

Major Bestler, the Military Attaché's office on the first floor.

"What do you think, Sir?" Sergeant Peacoe asked.

"Why would they send us a bomb expert?"

"A bomb expert? His 201 file says his last job was a clerk."

"Yeah, Peacoe, but did you read this, eight weeks demolition school, then another eight in Explosive Ordinance Disposal, training."

"Maybe he flunked out and that's why they made him a clerk." Sergeant Peacoe said.

"Not according to these Certificates, he graduated number one at demo school and top 5% at Lenordwood."

"I don't know, something is not right with this, we don't have a slot for a clerk typist and the kid doesn't have a security clearance or speak any languages." Peacoe said, trying to convince the Major that it was all some kind of mistake.

"I'll run it by the Ambassador this afternoon when he gets back. If he accepts him, we're going to keep him, this kid has a GT score of 130, and a two year college degree."

"What do I do with him in the mean time?"

"Call Gunny Berks and see if you can get him a bunk at the Security Detachment residence and send him up here, I want to meet him."

"Yes Sir, *Three Bags Full.*" That was Master Sergeant Peacoe's response any time he was given an order that he didn't agree with, or had objections to, but would carry out anyway. Peacoe left the Major's office to go back down stairs.

After meeting Major Bestler, I spent that afternoon in the Security Detachment barracks. The NCOIC, a Gunnery Sergeant Berks had put me in Staff Sergeant Ortega's room temporarily and told me to go get out of my *tacky khakis*, because the only military people who wear uniforms around the Embassy are the Marines, and even they wear civilian clothes when they are off duty and off the compound.

Sergeant Ortega was on leave, so I had the room to myself. I dug through my duffle bag and got out a dress shirt and a pair of slacks. I used the ironing board and iron that was in the utility room to knock the wrinkles out and changed clothes.

Staff Sergeant Posey answered the phone in the day room and came to tell me that Master Sergeant Peacoe wanted to see me in his office.

I walked back over to the main building, hoping that I was going to be able to stay here, but, if I was going to be reassigned, that was OK too. I just wanted to get settled somewhere, I was tired of living out of a duffle bag.

I knocked on the door to Sergeant Peacoe's office.

"Come in."

I opened the door and went in.

"Have a seat Specialist Whitley. I want you to go see the Security Officer, Mister Wellborn, he'll fix you up with a Embassy ID card, like this one." He motioned to the one he had clipped to his shirt pocket. "Wear it at all times when you are on the compound. He'll also start the paperwork on your security clearance."

"Does that mean I'm going to stay here?"

"Don't get your hopes up, the Ambassador says you're acceptable if we can get you into German classes, but I don't think that will be enough."

"Why not, Sergeant Peacoe?"

"Part of the Attaché Specialist's job is to transcribe documents from German to English, and the other way around. Do you really think you will be able to do that after a two week course in spoken German?"

"No Sergeant."

"That's right, no sergeant, I don't think so either, so I'm still short a man and there is no way I'm going to report you as filling the Attaché Specialist's slot. So that means not only I'm short a man but I don't have a job for you. The Major wants me to get you into the German class in Frankfurt, and to get you a security clearance, so, that's what I'm going to do, but, like I said, don't get your hopes up."

"Yes Sergeant, thank you Sergeant."

"Well, what are you waiting for? Didn't I tell you to go see the Security Officer?"

"Yes Sergeant." I said as I got up and left the office, I didn't have the nerve to ask him where Mister Wellborn's office was. I poked my head into the vending room to see if there was someone I could ask, but there wasn't anyone there so I walked down to the back stairs where the information directory was. Bingo there it is, Security Officer, First Floor, Room 107.

A Marine in uniform at the top of the stairs asked me where I was going, and pointed me in the right direction. I knocked on the door and was greeted by a young German woman.

"Can I help you?" She asked with only a slight accent.

"Yes, I'm suppose to see Mr. Wellborn about an Embassy ID Card, and doing some paper work about getting a security clearance."

"Mr. Wellborn is not here, but I can help you, have a seat and let me see your Military ID Card."

"Yes Ma'am." I said as I took out my ID Card and sat down in the chair beside her desk.

"Please don't call me Ma'am, call me Claire or

Mrs. Posey."

"Yes Ma'am, I mean Mrs. Posey. Are you related to Staff Sergeant Posey?"

"That's right, he's my husband. Can you stand against the wall, just there, so I can take your picture. Where are you going to be working?"

"Well, I don't know if I am. According to Sergeant Peacoe, he doesn't have a job for me, but the Major wants me to get stuff started, in case they can find one for me."

"That man Peacoe, I don't like him, he thinks he runs all the military people that work here. But in any case, I better give you a "C" pass for right now. I can always change it later when they figure out where you will be working." She said as she reached behind me and rolled up the blue background and pulled down a yellow one.

"A "C" pass?" I asked.

"All that means is that you will be restricted to the basement and the first floor. Don't ever go up stairs unless you are escorted. That would be a security violation and Mr. Wellborn frowns on those around here." She stepped back and took my picture with one of those instant cameras.

She talked to me, filling me in on some of the protocols and how things work around the Embassy, while I was filling out the personal history and background papers for my security clearance. When Major Bestler knocked then poked his head into the office.

"There you are Whitley, when you are finished here, come to my office for a minute." He didn't wait for a reply, he just popped back out and closed the door.

Claire continued telling me the ins and outs. She said that Donald, her husband, was required to keep a room in the residence hall, that's what they call the Security Detatchment's quarters, but that they have an apartment over on Wilhelm Levison Strasse. She told me that the two of the four guys with the DSS, (Diplomatic Security Service), who are the Ambassador's body guards, are ex-Marines, but most of the guys that worked for the Armed Forces Courier Service, which is also located on the compound, were active duty or ex-military personnel as well. She kept right on talking as I finish filling out the forms. She told me that the Ambassador was referred to as *Eagle*, his wife as *Birdie*, and their daughter as *Duckling,* the Chief Deputy as *Falcon,* the Embassy as *Perch*, the Ambassador's residence as *Nest* and the DSS guys as *Claw.*

"That's a lot to remember."

"No, you will get the hang of it. It's not really a code, just kind of a shorthand they use around here, like Birdie is on the Nest and Eagle is on the Perch. Be carefull though, don't get confused because there are some nicknames used that are not part of it, kind of an inside joke, you know, so don't repeat them.

"Like what?"

"Well they call Sergeant Peacoe, Peacock because he is always strutting around like he owns the place and Mr. Chilton, the Chief Deputy, some of the guys call him Sweet Pants, because, you know, he's not too manly. One other thing stay away from Mr. Connelly, the Chief Services Officer, he hates anything to do with the military and the guys just call him asshole. She finished talking, smiled, and handed me my new Embassy ID.

"Thank you Mrs. Posey, I'd better go see the Major now."

"Good luck Whitley, I hope they find a job for you.

"Thanks again, me too." I said as I got up and left the office and headed back down the halway to Major Bestler's office.

The door to the office was open and there was a man in an expensive looking suit standing in the doorway talking with the Major. I just stood there and waited for him to finish. When he did he just looked me up and down and left and the Major motioned me in and told me to shut the door.

"Do you have a tie?"

"Just my uniform tie, Sir."

"That won't do, here put this one on." He stood up and pulled one out of a bag of dry cleaning that was hanging on the coat rack in the corner of the office. "Any time you are up on the main floor make sure you are wearing a tie, it's required. I'll probably get a memo from Connelly, that's the guy that just left, avoid him like the plague."

"Yes Sir."

"Here is your letter of authorization to the finance office at Gibbs Kaserne in Frankfurt, they will give you $500, your initial clothing allowance. Buy a couple of consertive suits, a couple of sport coats, slacks, dress shirts, ties and a hat, make sure to buy a hat, the Ambassador hates to see bare heads in the winter time. Take a copy of this letter and a copy of your orders to the clothing sales store and they will issue you a set of dress whites, you will probably never wear them, but you are required to have them, if you want a set of dress blues, which is

14

recommended, you will have to buy them yourself."

"Yes Sir. When am I going to Frankfurt?"

"As soon as Sergeant Peacoe makes arrangements for you to attend the language school, there is a class starting next Monday, so you will probably leave Saturday.

"Does this mean I'm going to stay here?"

"Well, it means I'm working on it, but in the mean time you have orders assigning you here, so you might as well take advantage of the perks while you have the chance. How are the Marines treating you?"

"I've only met Sergeants Berks and Posey, I'll probably meet some of the other guys tonight."

"Good, you're situated then, for the time being anyway. The only people that live on the compound are the Marines, we'll have to work out something more permant when you get back from Frankfurt, if you are going to stay with us. Anyway, it may be premature, but welcome aboard."

"Thank you Sir, is there anything else."

"Just stay in the residence hall, so Master Sergeant Peacoe can find you when he has your travel authorization."

I had fallen asleep in the day room reading the Diplomatic Protocol Manual that I found on the bookshelf when I was awakened by Staff Sergeant Posey inspecting four of the Marines for guard change. Shortly after they left the guys that had been relieved came into the dayroom on their way to their rooms.

"Hey, look-a-here, new meat." Said one of the Marines.

"Nah, that's some Army dude, Jake and I saw him in the break room. Ain't that right Jake?" Said another.

"Yeah, that's right. What you doing in here man?"

"KNOCK IT OFF!" In came Staff Sergeant Posey. "This is Specialist Whitley, that's a Corporal to you clowns, he's going to be staying in Sergeant Ortega's room for a couple of days, and my Old Lady says he's OK, so fill him in on what's what, around here, and take him to chow with you, or she'll have your ass." Then Posey turned around and left.

The guys introduced themselves, and we were joined by four more guys that had been in their rooms, and went to the cafeteria that was located in the north wing basement of the main building. They serve a Continintial style breakfast, and a regular lunch for the Embassy employees, but after lunch the Chef goes to the Ambassador's residence to supervise the staff over there. The evening meal in the cafeteria is usually just for the Marines, the Embassy duty officer, and the night crew in the communications room. There is also a meal at midnight for the guys working, the night baker comes in at 2300 hours and whips up a big pan of scrambled eggs, bacon and potatoes.

Saturday, Sergeant Peacoe called me in to his office and gave me travel orders to Frankfurt and I caught a train that afternoon.

CHAPTER 2.

The Interview

I stayed at the transit barracks at 5th Corps Headquarters on Gibbs Kaserne. There was about twenty of us, but Peacoe was right, even if I caught on quick, there was not a chance in hell that I would be able to transcribe documents. The instructor, a Frau Giesell, made it clear the first day that there was a big difference between conversational and formal written German, but I enjoyed the class, tried hard and surprised myself as to how much I was picking up, it was fun. The fourth day we went on a field trip to the IG Farbin Building and went on a tour. The Tour Guide was quite capable of giving the tour in English, but Frau Giesell asked him go give it in German to get us familiar with the flow and tone of German speech instead of just learning words and phrases. We got the rest of the afternoon off when we got back from the tour, so I went to the clothing sales store, to pick up my dress whites, he didn't have any Specialist Four patches only Spec Fives, but he told me the tailor could cut the over bar off the patches when he hemmed the pants. I decided not to have any patches sewed on the jacket, like Major Bestler said, I would probably never get a chance to wear them. The next day was Saturday so I went shopping at the Main PX with Max Green and Joey

Seitz a couple of the guys in the class. When we got back to the Kaserne, we decided to go exploring and try our new found German. We located a Gasthaus down the street from the Kaserne and had a ball, our German wasn't perfect or anything like it, but we got by, ordering beer and dinner.

We went on field trips every other day after the first one, we learned how to read bus, streetcar, and train schedules and how to buy tickets. One of the trips was to the same Gasthaus that Joey, Max and I had already been to.

Two weeks flew by, and I was on my way back to Bonn, with my duffle and two fold over garment bags stuffed with new clothes. Can I speak German? Well, I can read a menu and order dinner, get a hotel room, find a latrine and get around on public transportation, but as far as being a German linguist, I have to say that Peacoe was right.

I met a British Captain named Martin on the train, and he asked me why I was going to Bonn. I told him I was stationed there and he thought that was strange since Bonn is in the British sector. I told him that I was maybe going to be stationed at the Embassy, and he told me that he was an acquaintance of Major Bestler. When we arrived there were a couple of *Red Hats*, that's what they call their MPs, there to pick him up and he offered me a ride to the compound.

I humped my bags around the back and down the stairs and reported in to Sergeant Peacoe.

"I've got some questions for you, soldier."

"Yes Sir, I mean Sergeant."

"When you left Fort Lenordwood, to go to Fort Sill, what did your orders say?" Peacoe asked as he looked over some papers in front of him.

"Just, Army Replacement Center, Fort Sill, Oklahoma."

"Well didn't you think it was a little strange that they sent you to an artillery unit."

"Yeah, maybe, but you've heard the stories, you know, a guy wants to drive a tank, so they send him to tanker school, then he ends up being a cook in an infantry unit."

"Well you should have said something to somebody."

"Look, Sergeant Peacoe, what was I going to say, and who would listen to me anyway, a PFC who had been in the Army less than a year."

"The answer I got from the message I sent to the personnel office at the, Department of the Army says you should have been assigned to the Ordinance Disposal Unit at Fort Sill.

"What does all this mean?"

"It means you got screwed, somebody fucked around with the assignments at the Replacement Center at Fort Sill, then you got screwed again when some dumb shit personnel clerk at the 2d of the 2d changed your MOS. The message also says your MOS has been changed again, this time to Duty Soldier."

"What the heck is a Duty Soldier?"

"It basically means that you are what ever the Army wants you to be, and you'll get on-the-job training when ever someone figures out where you are going to be assigned. But you have bigger problems then that. Mister Wellborn wants to see you, you have got some kind of a problem with your security clearance."

"What do I do now, Sergeant?"

"Wellborn is not in this afternoon, so I'm going to take you over to the Hoffstetter Hotel, and get you a room, that's where most of the single guys that work at the Embassy live. You have an appointment with Mr. Wellborn tomorrow at ten hundred hours, so grab your bags load them up in the blue Ford in the parking lot, and I'll be with you in about ten minutes. Here's the keys." He said as he pitched me the keys to the sedan.

It was more like twenty minutes, but I finally saw Peacoe walking down the sidewalk heading toward me while I was standing beside the sedan smoking a cigarette.

"Let's do it." He said and slid into the drivers side and I handed him back the keys. "That's something else you are going to have to do, if you stay around here."

"What's that Sergeant."

"Go over to the maintenance garage and see Smitty and get yourself a USAEUR drivers license. Well how was the school?" He asked me in German?

I thought I saw a bit of a smile, when I answered him in German, and told him I liked the school and the instructor, and I can speak a little but understand more.

"Not bad he said, but you're going to have to work on that Kentucky accent."

We pulled in to the Hoffstetter, it's an older hotel about three blocks from the Embassy. The bell man came out and helped me carry my bags in.

"Guten Tag Herr Peacoe, is this a new guest you have for us?" The man at the desk asked.

"Yes this is Herr Whitley, I'm not sure how

long he will be with us, but it will be the usual arrangements."

"Gut. Herr Whitley please sign here." The desk man said as he turned the register book around for me to sign, and got a key off the board and handed it to the bell man who was still standing there with my bags on a luggage cart. "Ein und zwanzig, Franz.

"Gut. Würden Sie bitte mit mir." Franz said as he tilted the luggage cart back and motioned for us to follow him.

Franz pulled the luggage into the ancient looking elevator, it had double collapsible iron gates instead of sliding doors. Peacoe motioned for me to follow him and we took the staircase and were already there when the elevator stopped.

"If I were you, I wouldn't use that elevator, it's slow and I don't trust it. I'm at the other end of the hall in 28 and you are going to be in room 21."

"Twenty one, yeah, I got that much. How long am I going to be here? I mean is this just temporary or going to be my quarters?"

Franz slid the gates open on the elevator and we followed him down the hall and waited for him to unlock the door.

"This will be your quarters if you are going to stay, Finance will deduct your quarters allowance. The married DPs (Diplomatic Corps Personnel), that have their wives with them have apartments on the economy, but the single guys live here."

Franz pulled the bags into the room and held the door for us then handed me the key.

"Should I?" I said as I looked at Peacoe and he was shaking his head no.

"Tips are included for residents." He already

knew what I was going to ask.

I took the key from Franz and said. "Danke schon."

"Bitte schon." Franz said as he took his luggage rack and left the room.

I looked around the room it was small, with a single bed and instead of a closet there was a wardrobe with double doors, I opened it, there was hanger space on the left with a shelf above that had towels and a bathrobe on it and drawers on the right hand side. A night stand by the bed had a ashtray and a table lamp on it, there was only one window with a hot water radiator below it. On the right side of the room was a sink and mirror with a small cabinet next to it and a waist paper basket under it. I looked at Peacoe.

"You passed it coming down the hall, the head is marked WC and the bath is marked Bade Zimmer. You can have a radio and a coffee pot, but absolutely no cooking in the room. In the morning there is coffee, juice, and sweet rolls down in the dining room, that is included in the cost of the room, but if you eat lunch or dinner you pay. When you go out in the morning leave your key at the desk, that's just the way they do things over here. Any questions?"

"No Sergeant, except how do I get to the Embassy in the mornings?"

"There is a carry-all that makes three trips every day except Sunday, the first pick up is 0700 and the last pick up is 0800, but a lot of the guys just walk unless it is raining. Is that it?"

"Yes Sergeant."

"Take the rest of the day off and have your ass in Wellborn's office at 1000 hours tomorrow."

"Yes Sergeant." I said as Peacoe left the room and shut the door behind him.

I looked around the room again, it was small but it was mine for the time being anyway, and a lot nicer than being in a barracks. I unpacked and hung up my new clothes, figured I would wear the brown sport coat and tan slacks for tomorrow. I should have asked him about dry cleaning and laundry, I thought to myself, but I didn't want to keep Peacoe any longer than necessary, I know he doesn't like me and is doing everything he can to get rid of me. I spent the afternoon exploring the neighborhood and spotted a Gasthaus named the *Idlehour* and equipped with my new German, went in and ordered a beer.

I slept good that night, the bed was soft and saggy just like the army beds I was used to. I got up early, shaved in my room then went down the hall to the shower. I got dressed and went down stairs and had a cup of coffee and a slice of what looked like a deep dish coffee cake. I was joined at the table by another American, a young guy in his early twenties, with curly red hair and a fair complexion. He didn't look very military so I figured he must be a clerk or something over at the Embassy.

"Hi, I'm Ernie, I work in the radio room. You the new guy?" He asked as he sat down at the table.

"Yep." I said. "Just call me Whitley, my first name is Ron, but since I've been in the Army. I've got used to just Whitley."

"I figured you were Army, if you were a Jarhead you'd be living over at the compound. I used to be in the Army, I was in ASA (Army Security Agency), did four years and never left the States.

"How did you end up over here, Ernie?"

"My brother is in the Diplomat Service and told me to apply for a job in communications since I never got a chance to leave the country when I was in the Army."

"Do you like it?"

"I love it, it's kind of like being in the Army, you know, you've got your big shots then you've got peons like me, and I'm doing about the same thing I was doing in the Army, radios and electronic communications gear, and the pay is a lot better. What about you?"

"Don't know yet, my orders said I was assigned to the Embassy but I don't think they have a job for me."

"Well I hope you get to stay. It would be great to have someone to hang out with, the three guys I work with are married and don't live at the hotel."

Wellborn's office, 0900 hours, the three men with Wellborn are DIS Agent Greevy, Defensive Investigative Service, and Chief Warrant Officer Novak, Armed Forces Courier Service, and Major Bestler.

"What, exactly is the problem with his clearance?" Bestler asked Greevy.

"It's not exactly a problem, it has to do with some of his step-father's family, it seems his step-dad has several brothers and the whole family is involved in organized crime. Three of the brothers have been killed, and three more are in prison."

"Christ, how many of them are there?"

Wellborn interjected.

"Ten brothers and a sister, plus in-laws, Jack, the boy's step-dad seems to be the only one that got away from it, when he moved to Kentucky, but then there is an FBI surveillance report on a Leo Antonelli, and a Paul Robinetti, he's the kid's uncle, and is the *Under boss* of the Long Beach "Family", that took over the Jack Dragna organization, and guess where they showed up four years ago?"

"I'm sure you're going to tell us." Bestler said with some skepticism.

"Kentucky, at Jack Robinetti's house."

"I'm sorry, but you just lost me. What does this have to do with Whitley? It just sounds like a guy visiting his brother." Wellborn asked starting to get annoyed with this scenario Greevy was building.

"Look, this isn't my idea, my orders are to conduct a personal interview with the guy to see why he didn't list any of his step-father's family on his personal history. You know, this is no joke, the Long Beach "Family" runs West Coast Cartage, which in turn controls the Teamster's and dock worker's Unions. Nothing moves in or off the west coast with out their OK, and that's not to mention using West Coast Cartage as a front for their criminal activities. Whitley was flagged as person of interest to the FBI when he joined the Army and was interviewed at Fort Sill when he was there. Now that he has applied for a security clearance, the powers that be, want to know why he didn't list Paul Robinetti as a relative of his."

"OK, I've got it now. You're here because he didn't list a relative of his, which is technically not a relative because it's his step-father's family. Is that right?" Major Bestler stated more that asked.

"And if he had listed this Paul Robinetti as a relative, you'd still be here. Is that right? Wellborn added sarcastically.

"Yeah, that's about it." Greevy said without understanding how ridiculous he sounded.

"Well I've heard enough of this crap. If you sign off on the kid's clearance, I want him and I have a job for him, so I'll let you guys figure it out." Chief Novak stood up and left the office.

"What time is Whitley suppose to be here?" Greevy asked.

"1000 hours. Let me know what you two decide. I'll be in my office." Major Bestler said as he also got up and left the room.

Ernie and I talked a while longer, especially about the local Frauleins, something Ernie seems to be obsessed with, and girls are something I haven't had much time to think about yet. We finished our coffee and walked to the Embassy, past the ever present line of people wanting to see the Services Officer. Americans with Passport problems or registering births and Germans wanting visas. Like I said we walked past the line at the north entrance and in the front door of the south wing for the first time for me. Jake was the Marine on duty.

"Looking good there Whitley." He said as a comment of the way I was dressed. I did look pretty sharp, even if I do say so myself.

"Thanks Jake." I replied as he passed us through the check point.

Ernie headed back to the south wing of the

building and since I was early, I went the other direction and down the stairs to check in with Sergeant Peacoe before going to my appointment. Peacoe's office was locked so I went on down to the break room and got another cup of coffee as I had about fifteen minutes to kill.

I knocked on the door and was greeted by Claire. She hit the button on the intercom and told Mr. Wellborn I was there.

"Send him in." Came the reply from the dark brown plastic box and Claire motioned for me to go through the door at the end of the office.

A middle aged, slightly balding, well dressed man stood up and extended his hand to me. "Specialist Whitley, I'm Chuck Wellborn the Embassy's Security Officer." We shook hands and he continued. "And this is Agent Greevy from the Defense Investigative Service, he has some questions about the personal history form you filled out for your security clearance, so have a seat."

Greevy didn't stand up or offer to shake hands, he just started in by handing me a copy of the form I had filled out about two weeks ago.

"Is that the personal history form you filled out?"

I thumbed through the four page document briefly and not seeing any mistakes I had made, replied. "Yes Sir."

"On page two under family members, you listed your brother and sisters then your father's family, then your mother's family, aunts uncles and so forth. Is that correct?"

"Yes Sir."

"Now on the next block, where it says "Other

family members not listed above." You have a Jack Robinetti born in Long Beach, California listed as your step-father. Is that correct?"

"Yes Sir."

"But you didn't list any of his relatives. Is that also correct?"

"Yes Sir."

"Why? I mean you listed all your aunts and uncles on your mother's and father's sides of the family, why not your step-father's?"

"Well, I didn't think it was necessary, and I don't know any of them."

"You've never met any of your step-father's relatives?"

"Well, let me correct that, I did meet my sisters' Grandmother, when she came out from California for a couple of days to see Jack and the girls, and I met one of Jack's brothers, my mother said to call him Uncle Paul, and a lady my mother said to call Aunt Roxanne came once on vacation and stayed a couple of weeks with us."

"Tell me about this Uncle Paul?"

"I don't know what you want me to tell you, I only met him once for a couple of hours."

"Just tell me the circumstances under which you met him."

"Well, it was early one morning when I was a kid, I woke up to laughter and some strange voices coming from downstairs. It was early in the morning and I looked out the window and saw a big black limousine and a fancy Cadillac convertible in the driveway. I went down stairs and Jack and Mom and four men in suits with their jackets off were sitting around the kitchen table laughing and drinking wine.

Mom told me that one of the guys was my Uncle Paul."

"Is there anything else you can tell me?"

"No, except two of the guys had guns in shoulder holsters, but I don't think they were cops, because one of them was a big fat guy, and he was the one that drove me to school that day and he had a funny name, like a girl, Sally or something like that."

"It seems to me that you have a pretty good memory of that day, why is that?"

"Well, it's not every day you get driven to school in a big black Cadillac limousine."

"Anything else you can tell me?"

"No Sir, that's it, I never saw them again, they were gone when I got home from school. I did ask my Mom why two of the guys had guns, and she told me it was because they were carrying a lot of money and going to the Kentucky Derby, and that's all I can tell you. Am I in some kind of trouble?"

"No Specialist Whitley, you're not in any trouble. That'll be all, Mr. Wellborn will let you know about your clearance in a couple of days."

Mr. Wellborn got up and walked me to the door and I waved at Claire as I left the office, she was on the phone and waved back.

"He doesn't know anything." Wellborn said.

"I agree with you, he doesn't even know who Leo Antonelli and Paul Robinetti are. I'll send my report in with a favorable." Greevy replied.

"Yeah, a big to-do about nothing. I'll let Bestler and Novak know, but we'll still have to wait for the clearance to come back."

CHAPTER 3.

To Catch a Spy

Office of Ian MacNally, Chief of Counter Intelligence, NATO Headquarters, Belgium. Behind the locked door of a secure briefing room, the Deputy NATO Commander is hearing for the first time about two serving Dutch Officers believed to be involved in espionage, also in attendance is Colonel Eric Goldman, Director of Intelligence for NATO.

"This is a new type of spy ring, at least a new one for us. Their motivation does not seem to be political, but simple, outright greed."

"How is this new then?" MacNally was interrupted by the Deputy Commander.

"They are being paid in opium, hundreds of kilos of opium, and are using aircraft on NATO training missions to evade customs and distribute the drugs throughout western Europe."

"This is unbelievable, how sure are you of this, and how many people are involved?" The Deputy Commander asked, visibly shaken by the information.

"The two Dutch Officers seem to be the key to the whole operation, but we don't have all the principles yet. We think there is a West German pilot stationed at Rhine Mien, and an American Air Force pilot stationed in Italy, and an American Naval

Officer stationed at Rhoda, Spain, involved in the distribution end, we don't think they know about the spying, just smuggling the drugs for money. As to the spy ring it self, we believe that low level Turkish Diplomats are involved in arranging for the transfer of the information and opium. Exchanges are made with the Dutch Officers using bags like this one." Ian MacNally said as he sat a bag upon the table.

"So you think the Turks are behind all this?"

"No Sir, the Russians. We think the Turkish diplomatic personnel are furnishing the opium for the Russians, specifically, our old friend Colonel Valerie Vilarian"

"Christ, not Vilarian again, that old fart has been dying of liver failure for the last ten years. How much and what type of information has been compromised"

"That we know of, Order of Battle plans for the American Armored Division units in the Fulda Gap, some missile strength and capability which we found references to before we got on to them. Air and submarine surveillance routes, which are not accurate, one of our operatives is in fact the person recruited by Squadron Commander Heiden, to furnish the information. Heiden is the senior of the two Dutch Officers, the other is a Captain Van Norge who works here in J2 Plans and we have been discreetly limiting the information he has access to. We may be able to turn Heiden, he has a wife and children, and a hell of a lot more to loose than Van Norge."

"Let me ask the obvious. Why don't you just shut the whole thing down, have the Military Officers arrested and turn the drug part of it over to the civilian authorities?"

"Yes Sir, of course that is an option, but if we can turn Heiden or Van Norge for that matter, it would give us a double agent in Vilarian's network. It would be better at this time if I turn the floor over to our own Spymaster, Colonel Goldman."

"OK Eric, let's hear your big plan."

"As you know Sir, since you were my predecessor, we have been trying to get into Vilarian's spy network for many years. Turning Heiden or Van Norge or both, would give us the key to do what no western intelligence agency has been able to do, not the British, not the CIA or the West Germans, not even us until now, and that is put our man or men right inside the biggest spy operation the Russians have assembled since World War II."

"Say you can turn Heiden but not Van Norge or the other way around, what happens then?"

"The one that doesn't turn will have to be eliminated."

"Christ. Eric, you're not saying what I think your saying."

"No Sir, of course not, but we can filter information to, say, the Spanish National Police that he is a major drug smuggler, and make arrangements for them to find him in Spain, with the evidence of course. A little money in the right place and even the Russians won't be able to get to him in a Spanish jail."

"OK, say that works, how do you get out of the opium smuggling business and get your man inside?"

"That's the easy part." Goldman said with a smirk of self-assurance."

"OK, continue."

"We include a note to the Russians in the

microfilm, saying that he wants to get out of the opium business, because it is getting too dangerous, and that he is being reassigned to, let's say a sensitive area that the Russians won't be able to resist. He would be willing to work directly with the Russians for money because he doesn't trust the Turks anymore because he thinks the police have an informant inside the drug operation. Which in fact is true, we have a man inside the Turkish network, that is where we are getting some of our information. What do you think?" Goldman asked with that same smirk of self assurance.

"There is a hundred things that we know of that could go wrong, then there is always the unexpected, but it could work."

The Deputy Commander is on the hook just as MacNally and Goldman thought he would be after they explained the plan, but they still need his official approval.

"Tell me again, what happens to the Turks and the smuggling ring, you can't just leave them in place, I mean they are not just going to go away. As soon as the Russians pull out of the deal, they will just convert to a cash business, I mean they are the ones providing the opium, as I understand it."

"Yes Sir, of course, we have planned for that event. When the Dutchmen and the Russians are out of the equation, we, through discreet contacts, give everything on the drug operation to the British or the American CID and let them call in INTERPOL and let INTERPOL take over the lead and coordinate with all the civilian law enforcement agencies involved. It will be strictly a police matter and we will be three times removed from the whole deal."

"Dangerous, very dangerous, not to mention the black eye we'll take when the military officers involved are arrested."

"Not so much us, as the individual country's and their armed forces, and I think we can rely on our brothers in CID to minimize the repercussions on their level."

"Anything else, there is always something else. What haven't you told me?"

MacNally turned to Goldman as if to say, I told you so, then Colonel Goldman finally spoke up and the smirk on his face was gone.

"There is one other player, we only know as "The Finn", we don't know who he is or what he looks like. We do know he fits somewhere between the Turks and the Dutchmen, but what he does or how important he is, we just don't know yet. We hope to get that information from Heiden or Van Norge."

"And how did you come by this information?"

"Our man with the Turks."

"Anything else?"

"If you approve the operation, we plan on bringing Günter Schmitt in from Italy to run the field operation, if that meets with your approval."

"That's fine, Günter is a good man." The Deputy Commander said as he reminisced for a moment about the time he worked with Günter in North Africa, then continued. "Well, what are we going to call this operation?"

"Norseman." Ian MacNally spoke up.

"Why Norseman?"

"Norseman is a now defunct, dummy operation that was set up to feed the Russians wrong information about Spitsbergen submarine surveillance routes, so if the Russians pick up any information on Norseman they will assume it has to do with an operation that they know is a fake and ignore it."

"OK, Operation Norseman it is. I'll want another briefing tomorrow, on the resources and money you'll need, then weekly briefings there after. Oh, and Eric, if this thing goes bad, I would think about retiring if I were you. Understand?"

"Yes Sir." Goldman replied as the Deputy Commander got up to leave the room.

CHAPTER 4.

A Home at Last

After the interview with Agent Greevy and Mr. Wellborn, I went back down stairs to check in with Sergeant Peacoe, and see if he had anything for me to do.

"Have a seat Whitley, I'll be with you in a second." Peacoe continued on with his phone call.

"Yes Sir.........."Yes Sir."........."Don't you think we're pushing this a little?"........."Yes Sir, I understand." Peacoe hung up the phone and mumbled "three bags full" to himself then looked in my direction. He wasn't looking at me, just in my direction thinking about something. I could almost see the gears turning around in his head. Finally he spoke.

"OK Whitley, here is what I want you to do. After lunch, I want you to go to the maintenance garage and see Smitty, pick up a driver's manual, go back to your room and study it this afternoon, and tomorrow morning go back and take your drivers test, then go to the building next to the shop and report in to Mr. Novak, you will be working for him in the office until your clearance gets back. Any questions?"

"No Sergeant."

"Well, what are you waiting for? Get out of

here, and don't slam the door."

"Yes Sergeant." I said as I got up and left, and wondered to myself, does Peacoe really not like me, or is he just trying to be a hard ass.

As I got back to the garage area there was a couple of guys washing cars, one of which was the Ambassador's Lincoln. I found Smitty in the office he was a short, dark haired fellow and friendly enough, but not exactly a picture of Arian manhood. He told me he did all the vehicle maintenance on the compound and used to have an assistant, but it was easier for him to just do the work himself. He gave me a manual to study and told me to make sure I had fifty marks with me tomorrow, and after he issued me a visiting forces driver's license, he would take me over to the Bonn City Hall and get me an international license.

I took the long way around the circular drive past the building I would report in to tomorrow, but there was no sign out front, then on past the tall iron gate where the drive forked, the gate was locked, then the wall that separated the Ambassador's residence from the rest of the compound. The residence has its own entrance and driveway on the main street, but is still part of the compound. Another break in the wall with an iron foot gate. I suspect this is the path the Ambassador takes going back and forth. I left the compound through the vehicle gate and walked back to the hotel. I studied the driving manual, mainly learning to recognize the international traffic signs, until about 1700 hours, when I received a knock on my door. It was Ernie, and he offered to show me some of the city. We caught a strassenbahn (streetcar) on the main drag and headed down to the square where the bahnhof (train station) is located. We walked and talked for awhile and came to a gasthaus, but Ernie said a lot of off duty British soldiers went there and they could get pretty rowdy sometimes. We walked a couple of blocks more to another place that Ernie likes to go, and there was a four man *ump pa* band playing and everyone was having a good time. We had dinner and a few beers and stayed about three hours then headed back to the hotel.

The next morning I passed my drivers test, then Smitty took me to town and I got my international license. On the way back he told me he had been working at the Embassy for nine years and started as the assistant mechanic and couldn't speak a work of English when he started. He also told me he is married and has a son at the University of Heidelberg studying to be a Doctor.

When we arrived back, I thanked him for his help and walked to the building next door. It was a modern single story brick building, and I went in the double doors at the center of the building and there were three more doors. The door straight ahead wasn't marked, but the one on the left read: DIPLOMATIC COURIER'S OFFICE. Directly across the small hall the door read: ARMED FORCES COURIER SERVICE. Sergeant Peacoe didn't tell me which one, so I took a guess and knocked on the one on the right.

"Come in." The voice said from the other side of the door, as I opened it and went in.

The man behind the desk was on the telephone and motioned for me to sit down. The name plate on his desk read CWO James Novak, Station Chief. He looked to be in his mid to late thirties and had a hard, rugged look about him with a small scar on his chin and was wearing a dress shirt with the top button undone and a tie loosened around his neck. I just sat there and waited for him to finish on the phone. He put his hand over the bottom part of the receiver. "Help your self to a cup of coffee and I'll be with you in just a minute." He said as he motioned to the open door on his right, then went back to his conversation.

The large room had a desk facing out from the left hand corner with three telephones on it, identical to the ones on Novak's desk, and kitchen cabinets with a sink and coffee pot in the right and door in between the two. There was a large table with several chairs around it, a large map and a chart board on the wall. I was just stirring some cream into my coffee when he joined me in the room.

"That's OK, just have a seat at the table. You're Specialist Whitley, right?" He said as he poured himself a cup and sat down across from me.

"Yes Sir, Sergeant Peacoe told me I would be working here for awhile."

"How old are you son?"

"Nineteen Sir."

"Well to start with you can drop the Sir, we're informal around here. I'm Jim Novak or if it makes you feel more comfortable, you can call me Mr. Novak. Nineteen, wow, I don't think we have ever had anyone stationed here as young as you, but I'm going to put you to work. Is that alright with you?"

"I'm ready, what am I going to be doing, all Sergeant Peacoe said is that I'll be helping out in the office."

"I'm going to start you off on the duty phone,

while Sergeant Kersie is on leave. It is simple enough, you just answer the phone and write down what they tell you and when you are not on the phone, which is 99% of the time you can type up and file the logs, and an occasional letter for me."

"Yes Sir, I can handle that."

"Good come on and I'll show you how it works. First of all this is the duty board. As you can see we have four assignments working. "T" assignments are transporting classified or sensitive documents. "E" assignments are escort duty. The couriers won't give you a name on the phone. All the jobs are assigned a working name, that's the first column on the board, the second is the courier's name, then the start location, then the drop or final location. So the caller will give you two words then one or two phonetics, you repeat the two words and the phonetics back and he will hang up. The first word will be the working name of the job and the second word will be the city he is calling from and the phonetics will be the mode of transportation, from this list." He said pointing to the board then continued. "So if the caller says, *Violet, Paris, Charlie Alpha*, what would that mean?"

"Violet is the job, the courier is currently in Paris and will be departing by commercial air. Is that correct?"

"Good, you've got it. Now if the caller gives you the job name then says *Bosco*, that means the job is complete and he is currently at the final location. Now if you have another job waiting say *Call your mother* and the courier will call back on the scrambler, that's the red phone. That may take some time because he will have to get to a phone where he can use his portable unit. If he has been requested to make a pick up, he will tell you he has to call his mother. Still OK?"

"Got it."

"Don't worry about the red phone if I'm here, I'll take care of it. If you do have to answer it, just pick up the receiver and you will hear four beeps then you will hear four answering beeps on the other end, then wait for the caller to start talking. The duty phone is the white one, and the black one is just the regular office phone. You answer the duty phone by just saying 4956, that's the last four numbers of the phone. The office phone just answer, Armed Forces Courier Service. Any questions so far?"

"No sir, not yet."

"Good, I think you'll be able to handle it. I come in at eight and leave at six, you'll come in at 10 and work till eight when you are relieved by one of the night duty officers. We knock of at noon on Saturdays, the duty officer will come in and work till midnight then the phones are transferred to the com center on the first floor of the north wing, so on Mondays stop by and pick up any Sunday logs. Any questions?"

"I'm sure there will be, but I don't know what they are yet."

"Don't worry, I'll be here with you most of the time, and you'll get the hang of it."

As it happened, of course, I didn't get my first call on the duty phone until five minutes after Novak left for lunch, but it was a simple call-in in route, so I just logged it. It didn't take long to get comfortable with the job over the next few days. I liked the slow pace at first, then it started to get a little boring, but I felt lucky to be here, even if it is only till Sergeant Kersie gets back from leave.

I've learned my way around town and enjoyed exploring on my own or with Ernie. Ernie finally met a girl that would go out with him. Her name was Edletroud but Ernie called her Eddy and sometimes on Sundays she would bring one of her girlfriends for me and we would all go out for the day. The girls talked so fast and used a lot of slang so it was hard for me to keep up with the conversation. Oh they understood me ok, but I only caught about twenty percent, especially when they were talking with each other. One Saturday afternoon Eddy brought along a girl named Anna, we went out for dinner then to a little beer stub and talked for hours. Anna was not anymore attractive than the other girls, but there was just something about her that I really liked. Unfortunately she was leaving to go back to university, so I wouldn't get a chance to see her again, at least not for a while.

My clearance had come in and it was for Top Secret, not that anybody was going to tell me any secrets, that is, but it was one step closer to being able to stay here. I was in the office one day when a tall lady walked in, she was not exactly what you would call a looker.

"Can I help you?"

"Who are you and where is Mother?"

"Mr. Novak will be back in about an hour, he's at a meeting. Can I help you with something?

"I'm Sergeant Kersie, who are you again?"

"Oh, Sergeant Kersie, I didn't know you are a-"

"Are a what? I'm a Sergeant First Class, and let me slow it down for you. Who---Are---You?"

"I'm sorry, Sergeant Kersie, I'm Specialist Whitley."

"You're sorry you are a Specialist, or a Whitley, or both?"

"I mean, I'm sorry I didn't know who you are."

"Why, we've never met before. Now do you want to tell me what you are doing here?"

"Yes Ma'am, I mean Sergeant. I'm working the duty phone while you are on leave."

"So I go on leave and you think you can just come in here and take my job. Is that it?"

I didn't know what to say and about that time in came Mr. Novak and Bill Wilson, one of the couriers, they were both laughing.

"Had you going, didn't I?" Sergeant Kersie said with a smile on her face.

Yeah they got me, it was all in good fun, but now that Kersie is back, I didn't know if I still had a job.

"Well, Whitley. What are we going to do with you?" Novak asked.

"I don't know." I said as the office phone rang and Sergeant Kersie answered it and I got up to let her sit down at Novak's desk.

"You do like it here, don't you?"

"Yes Sir."

"And you would like to stay?"

"Yes Sir."

"Well then, starting tomorrow night, you'll be one of the night duty officers, Jerry is going on leave and Sammy is going to be reassigned back to Washington in a couple of months. Do you think that will suit you?"

"Yes Sir." I said and was happy to still have a

job.

"OK then, finish out your shift today and tomorrow come in at 2000 hours. Sammy will work with you the first night, not that you need it, but he will show you the routine just incase."

"I knew the job would be easy, but easy also meant boring, and boring means the time passes slow while you are on duty. Both Jerry and Sammy are DOD, that's Department of Defense civilians, and until Jerry went on leave, I only worked every third night then every other night. The only break in the routine was Saturday night at midnight, you had to call over to the communications center and have the duty line and the secure line switched over, then go over to the main building and use the red phone to call one of the other stations to confirm that the lines were switched over and working. We would also use the red phone to call another station at the beginning of each shift to do a com check and verify that the scrambler was working correctly. The rest of the time you just sat around the office reading or working cross word puzzles waiting for the phone to ring. In the small room off to the side of the large office was a bunk, and if you were a light sleeper you could catch a two hour nap between 0300 and 0500. It wasn't so bad if you had something to occupy your time, I did a lot of reading, the bookcase in the same room with the bunk was packed with paperbacks.

About seven weeks had passed and I was hoping that I would take Sammy's place when he left, but his replacement arrived a couple of days beforehand, so I was on the verge being without a job again. It was my last night on duty and I was about to get the hotplate out of the cabinet and make some canned soup when the front door buzzer went off, so I went to the front, opened the office door and looked down the short hall and could see Ernie's head through the glass in the door. I walked over and unlocked the door.

"Here." He said as he handed me a lunch bag, then continued. "I was filling in for one of the guys and just got off, so I went down to midnight chow and figured you might be hungry."

"Hey thanks a lot."

"No problem. Well I've got to work again in the morning so I'm going to bed, but before I forget. Eddy and I are going over to the British army Kaserne to see a movie Sunday, and she wants to know if you'll go with us, because she has a girlfriend that wants to go too."

"Yeah, it sounds good to me."

"OK, Sunday then, about noon." He turned to leave, got a few steps then said over his shoulder. "You didn't even ask what she looks like." Then kept walking.

I locked the door then looked in the bag, it was a couple of bacon and egg sandwiches and that sounded better than a can of soup.

The next morning, Mr. Novak told me to come back about 1600 hours and he might have some news for me. At least that was some hope and better than him coming right out and telling me I was out of a job. I walked back to the hotel, stopped at the desk to get my room key and pay for some dry cleaning that was back. That reminded me that I still hadn't returned Major Bestler's tie so I got it out of the drawer it was in and set it out so I wouldn't forget it this afternoon. I set my alarm clock and crashed out.

That afternoon I didn't forget the tie again, it was still in the dry cleaning sleeve so I tucked into my inside pocket. I had plenty of time so I went down the hall and knocked on the door then went in. Major Bestler was at his desk and told me to have a seat. I told him I just had a minute and wanted to return the tie he lent me. I handed it to him and apologized for not returning it sooner.

"Well, how do you think you are going to like your new job?"

"What job sir?"

"You haven't talked to Jim Novak yet?"

"No Sir, I'm on my way over there now."

"Oops. I better let Jim tell you."

There was another knock at the door, it was one of the ladies that works in the typing pool, so I excused myself and I got up and left the office to head over to see Mr. Novak. I walked into the office and Sergeant Kersie was at the front desk.

"Mother wants to see you in the back." She said as she motioned toward the closed door of the work room.

I immediately knew something was up, because that door is usually open, and as soon as I opened the door I saw Mr. Novak, two of our couriers, Don Wilson one of the diplomatic couriers and Jerry one of the night duty officers, then Kersie followed me into the room.

"Whitley, you know the regulations say that couriers have to be at least 21 years old. Well in your case I requested a 13 month age waiver, and with the help of letters of recommendation from Major Bestler and Mr. Wellborn, you have been approved. Whitley you have found a home."

"You won't be seeing much of it, but congratulations anyway." Danny Spalding, one of our couriers added.

He was joined by the rest of the guys in the room offering their congratulations. Then Mr. Novak spoke up.

"Tomorrow, I want you to go over and see the passport services officer, and he'll do the paper work and order your Diplomatic Passport, it will have to come from Washington, so it will come in the pouch in about six days."

"I'll make sure it's in there on my next trip." Don Wilson added.

"In the mean time Danny will take you over to the British Kaserne and get you qualified on a small frame 38. Well are you happy?"

"Yes Sir."

"Well, you may not be when I tell you the rest. If you lose your weapon, you may lose your job. If your scrambler case gets lost you may go to jail. Questions?"

"No Sir."

"OK then, when all the "I"s are dotted and all the "T"s crossed you'll go with Danny on a job, then you go on the board."

"That Sunday I was pleasantly surprised to find out my date for the day was Anna. I don't know if it was me she wanted to go out with again or the movie we were going to see, but it didn't make any difference to me, I was sure we would have a good time. We took the strassenbahn to the end of the line then caught a bus to the Kaserne. There was some confusion at the gate. The Sergeant didn't want to let us in and called for the duty officer, but before he arrived Captain Martin, the officer I met on the train that gave me a ride to the Embassy, came through the gate and stopped and signed us all in. The movie was "Blowout", the girls had already seen the movie in German, but wanted to see it in English, because there was some kind of controversy about the film and wanted to see if the German dubbing matched the English dialog. The girls were intellectuals and really enjoyed long discussions about trivial stuff like that. Beer and conversation seems to be the main pastime for the young in Germany.

After the movie we took the bus and streetcar back to town and had dinner and more conversation then took a walk around town then put the girls on their streetcar and said good-bye. It was a thoroughly enjoyable Sunday afternoon.

Five days later I did my first job with Danny Spalding, it was the regular US Army Europe Headquarters run, that did a *Round Robin* that started at USAREUR then made drop-offs and pick-ups at all the major Military units in Europe then back to the Headquarters. It was two long days and nights with cat naps on the trains then back to Bonn. Danny let me do all the check-ins and told me that we always try to make the run in two days, but if you get delayed and are running behind it is best to spend the night in Italy then get an early start. He also told me that there is another USAREUR run that goes to London and Washington DC that used to be handled by the Washington D.C. station but we are going to be picking it up. I was tired when we got back to Bonn and Danny told me I'd get use to it. Danny went to the office to report in and I went straight to the hotel to go to bed. When I got to my room I found that a telephone had been installed, but what I was interested in was a shower and bed.

CHAPTER 5.

The General's Wife

NATO Headquarters, Günter Schmitt is briefing Ian MacNally and Colonel Eric Goldman on Operation Norseman and his plan to turn Squadron Cmdr. Heiden.

Günter Schmitt is a short unimposing man that is very soft spoken and his appearance and mannerisms often mislead people, that don't know him, as to his sharp crafty mind.

"We have not been able to develop any more information on *The Finn,* but we are ready to approach Heiden and I should have the results the next time we meet."

"What exactly are you waiting on?" MacNally asked.

"Well as you know, we have taps on both of their telephones, and have monitored a call between Heiden and Van Norge about a meeting that has been set up, we don't know with whom the meeting is with or the subject, so we are going to wait and see what information we can gather, before approaching Heiden."

"Well Günter, tell me, what are your plans if after approaching Heiden, he flatly refuses to cooperate or denies his involvement?" Goldman asked.

"In that case, he will have to be immediately eliminated."

London, Office of Sir William Benchley, Director of Special Operations, for the British Home Ministry.

Captain Martin has been summoned from Germany and has no idea what this meeting is about as he waits in Benchley's outer office. He knows it can't be good, because he has done *special* jobs for Benchley's predecessor.

"Captain Martin you can go in now." The secretary said.

Martin entered the private office and was told to have a seat. He assumed the man behind the big desk was Benchley, but there was another man in the room, and no introduction was offered.

"Captain Martin, I see you are former SAS and were reclassified because of a back injury, is that correct?" The unidentified man spoke.

"That is correct - may I ask?"

"Yes, yes, we'll get to that. You are fit for duty, correct, I mean it doesn't affect your normal activities, you are not infirmed or any such thing, are you?"

"No more parachuting, but other than that, I'm fit."

"You have done *special* work for the Crown before. Do you feel up to an assignment similar to the job you did in Lebanon?"

"I'm a Serving Officer, I assume that such

orders are necessary, and I follow them."

"Good, good. Well then, do you know who this is?" The man handed Martin a photograph.

"No."

"Do you know who Sean O'Finn is?"

"Of course. He's a child murdering IRA bastard."

"Well that is a photograph of O'Finn, and besides the school bus in Inneskellen and the assassination of four RUC Constables, there is a club bombing here in London and a Police Station in Liverpool and that is only what we can prove."

"If O'Finn is my target, surely you can put him in prison for the rest of his life. Why would you want me to handle it?"

"The problem with a public trial, is that it is *public*, and there is some very sensitive and embarrassing information that could come out at a trial."

"What you mean is, the bloody bastard was working for you."

"Correct, at one time O'Finn was a paid informant, suppose to be working for us inside the IRA, until we realized that the information he was giving us was total rubbish. You see that kind of information being released at a trial is not an option."

"I have no problems with handling the murdering bastard, one of the children on the school bus was a niece of mine."

"I'm sorry, we didn't know that." Sir William Benchley spoke up for the first time.

"He is working out of the Frankfurt area, but has been spotted several times by the French drug police, in Paris and Marseilles and they are trying to identify him, that is where this photograph came from. We have sent an Inspector from Scotland Yard to Paris to work with the French police since they believe that the man they are trying to identify is from the UK. The inspector, however, is instructed not to tell them who O'Finn is, but to keep us informed on what he is up to, and his movements."

"Is the Inspector my contact?"

"NO. The Inspector knows nothing about you. We will give you as much information as possible on O'Finn's location. Since you are stationed in Germany, we would prefer that you did the job in France, if possible."

Back in Bonn.

My new telephone rang and I answered it. I must of went out as soon as I hit the bed, anyway it was Mother, and he told me to come in and be ready to be gone for 3 or 4 days. I cleaned up packed and got dressed and headed to the office.

Well my first job on my own was not what I expected, it was an escort assignment. I had to take a train to Frankfurt and pick up a Major General's wife and escort her to a private rehab clinic in Houston, Texas.

"Listen Whitley, you keep a close eye on this lady, the last time they tried to send her, she got away from the Lieutenant they sent with her, and they found her a week later in a French jail with no money or identification. She would probably still be there if she hadn't sobered up enough to tell the American

Consul who she was. Any questions?"

Novak asked and I could tell he didn't want to send me on this job, being the first one on my own, but there was no one else. Danny had already left to make a pick-up, and two of the couriers were in the middle of runs and the other two were on mandatory down time.

"Where do I pick her up and what is my authority to restrain her if she doesn't want to cooperate."

"Here is a letter from her husband, a letter signed by two of her doctors, and a letter from USAREUR Headquarters revoking her dependant status in Europe. This is your point of contact at the clinic, they are expecting her. Pick her up at V Corps Headquarters at Gibbs Kaserne."

"Anything else I need to know?"

"At least you are not going to be alone. There is a female MP at the General's headquarters that is due to rotate back to the States and she is going to be accompanying you. Your courier credentials came in, and here is your open travel orders and your authorization to draw up to 14 days per diem at any military finance office.

"When do I leave?"

"Right now, Kersie will take you to the train station, and Whitley, just in case." Novak said as he slid a pair of handcuffs with a key across the desk. "Only if it is absolutely necessary."

I got off the train and took a taxi to the headquarters and I was expecting some kind of raving lunatic. I was wrong Mrs. Camber was quite refined, and gentile. She must have been a beautiful woman when she was younger, and was still quite attractive even though she was a bit beyond her prime. I had passed the MP in the General's outer office, she was a young buck Sergeant, and so-so in appearance. I thought about asking her to change into civilian clothes, but re-thought that, it was probably better if she was in uniform, just in case. I left them alone to say their good-byes and waited in the outer office with the MP.

"Your first name is not Jessie is it?" I asked as I looked at her name tag which read JAMES.

"No it isn't." Is all she said without offering to tell me her first name. Oh well, I thought to myself, this could be a long trip.

"Here hang on to these, I don't think we will need them, but just in case." I handed her the handcuffs and key, I mean I was already packing enough stuff.

As it turned out, it was a long trip before we even got on the plane. First our flight was delayed for 30 minutes then another 45 minutes then cancelled altogether, there was something wrong with the aircraft. They finally came up with another plane and by the time we took off we were five hours behind schedule. Sergeant James and Mrs. Camber were deep in conversation about their families and I dozed off for a few moments and was awakened by Mrs. Camber trying to order a Vodka Martini from the Flight Attendant but Sergeant James handled the situation, and after we gave her our dinner choices I went back to my nap until the meal arrived. The ladies both had the beef tips and a salad, and I had the fish and pasta salad. It's not that I thought the fish was the best choice, was something Mr. Novak told me. "When ever there are two of you on an assignment, always order different meals, just in case." He didn't say in case of what, but he didn't have to.

After dinner, Sergeant James took out Mrs. Camber's medication she was carrying and gave her a couple of pills to take, then she said she needed to visit the little girls room. I figured it would be a good idea if we all went. While Mrs. Camber was taking care of business and Sergeant James was waiting out side the door, I took the opportunity to explain to the senior flight attendant our peculiar situation. When Mrs. Camber was finished I took her back to her seat and waited for the Sergeant to return. When she did, I went and managed to snag a coffee on the way back. It wasn't long after everyone had settled down in the cabin that they dimmed the lights and started the movie. *Cabaret* with Liza Minnelli, now there's a movie to sleep through. It wasn't long and the ladies were asleep and by the end of the movie almost everyone on the plane had joined them. I eased out of my seat and went to find another cup of coffee, I figured one of us needed to stay awake, but I did manage to get a couple of cat naps in.

About an hour before we were due to land in Miami the lights came back up and the flight attendants came through with coffee and soft drinks. It was nine in the evening when we finally landed. My credentials got us by customs with out any hassle. There was a flight to Houston at eight in the morning and another one at eleven thirty. I got us tickets for the eleven thirty flight and had the airlines book us two rooms at one of the airport hotels. We took the shuttle bus to the hotel and checked in. I had left 8 AM wake up calls for the rooms and told the girls we would have breakfast in the morning before we left.

I called the room the next morning to make sure they were up. Sergeant James answered the phone and said Mrs. Camber was taking a shower, and I told her I'd meet them in the restaurant downstairs in thirty minutes. I checked out and asked the desk clerk to send a bell man up to their room for the bags. I was having coffee in the restaurant waiting for the ladies to come down and thinking so-far so-good, except for the flight being five hours late, missing our connecting flight, and the martini incident on the plane Then when Sergeant James walked in the restaurant and I didn't see Mrs. Camber, I got a sick feeling in the pit of my stomach.

"Where is she?"

"When I got out of the shower, the bags were gone and so was she, so I figured she was with you."

"She can't go far, she doesn't have any money. Does she?" I asked.

Sergeant James opened her purse and said. "Oh shit, not only does she have money but she has her passport, check book and drivers license.

"OK, get all the bags and head to the airport departure building. Here's a five for the bellman and five for the Skycap, you hang on to the tickets. I'm going to make some calls and I'll meet you in the departure lounge.

After talking with the desk clerk, and finding out he saw her get on the shuttle, I had him get Airport Security on the phone for me.

"Lieutenant Sanchez, my name is Whitley, I'm an Armed Forces Courier on escort duty and I've lost my package. - Yes. - She is about 5'6", bottle blond hair, early forties, fairly attractive, well dressed. -

Yes. Just a second."

"Did you notice what she was wearing?" I asked the Desk Clerk."

"Blue dress, heels and a black bag, "

"Did you get that?" - Yeah, blue dress high heels and a black bag, her name is Irene Camber and Lieutenant Sanchez she's a alcoholic. Is there anything open this early for her to get a drink? ..... Yes sir, I have custody authorization and letters from her doctors. ..... Yes sir, I'm on my way and there is a female MP named James, that should be arriving at the departure terminal any time now."

I didn't wait for the shuttle, I grabbed a cab and headed to the airport. When I got to the departure terminal I stopped the first Security Officer I saw and had him call Sanchez on the radio. They had her at the airport lounge waiting for the bartender to open up. When I arrived at the lounge Sanchez and two other officers were there as well as James who had Mrs. Camber in handcuffs.

"Thanks for your help Lieutenant, we can handle it from now."

"Are you sure, she looks pretty dangerous to me."

"Yeah, and thanks again for your help."

"You know, I wasn't going anywhere, I just, you know, wanted one more before I checked in."

Sergeant James dumped Mrs. Camber's bag out on one of the seats and retrieved her passport, identification and the money she had taken from her bag.

"Well Mrs. Camber, have you gotten all this foolishness out of your system, or do we have to keep you handcuffed all the way to Houston?"

"No, I'm done, no more games I promise."

"OK, Sergeant un-cuff her."

"But Mr. Whitley." Sergeant James protested.

"It doesn't make any difference anyway Sergeant, she can't wear the cuffs on the plane."

It was almost ten and the lounge was opening for business, so since we missed breakfast, I decided that we would just get an early lunch right here. After we ate we walked on down to our gate to wait for check in time.

The flight to Houston was uneventful, and we took a taxi to the clinic, it was about a thirty minute ride from the airport, and Mrs. Camber was true to her word, there was no more misbehaving. I asked the director of the clinic if there was a room where I could make a private phone call and she said I could use her office. I opened my briefcase and got my FTS (Federal Telephone System) directory out and looked up the number for the FTS Operator in the Houston area, gave her my authorization number and told her I needed to call a number in West Germany and gave her the phone number to the duty phone. She told me to stand by it would take a moment or two. I waited on the phone for about 20 seconds then heard a dial tone then heard the operator dial the number and when the phone answered she said go ahead sir.

"Rainbow, Bosco." I said.

Then I heard Mr. Novak's voice on the other end. "Confirm Rainbow, Bosco, Call your mother."

"Roger, I'll call my mother right now."

I hung up then redialed the FTS Operator and gave her the number to the secure phone, then placed the hand set into the portable scrambler in my briefcase and put the ear piece in my ear. I heard the four beeps then my unit beeped four time.

"Is that you Whitley?" I heard Mr. Novak ask.

"Yes Sir, it's me."

"How did things go?"

"She's delivered, no complaints."

"Good, Good, I've got a pick-up for you. Fly to D.C., your job is at the Pentagon Room E104, your job name is Redbird, and you are going to the Office of the Deputy Commander, NATO, *eyes only*. Understand?"

"Yes Sir. Redbird, Pentagon Room E104, NATO, Deputy Commander, *eyes only*."

He hung up the phone and I heard two beeps then my portable beeped twice. I turned the unit off and hung up the phone.

I thanked the Director for letting me use her office and she walked me back out to the front desk. Mrs. Camber had already been taken back for her in processing. I asked the receptionist to call another taxi for me and offered Sergeant James a ride to the airport. James told me she needed to go to the bus station and I said no problem.

"Downtown Houston bus station then to the airport." I told the driver as he was putting our bags in the trunk.

I was glad to have Mrs. Camber off my hands and was looking forward to making my pick-up at the Pentagon and heading back to Europe.

"It's Lisa by the way."

"What's that?"

"Lisa, my name, you asked but I didn't tell you, I figured you would ask again, but you never did."

"Oh. Lisa, that's a good name." What a stupid

thing to say, but I was tired and wasn't in the mood for conversation, besides the time we were going to spend together was over and this was not the time to start up something new, there wasn't a chance in hell that we would ever see each other again.

The taxi pulled up to the bus station and the driver got out to open the trunk. I leaned over to the open door and said. "Good luck, Sergeant Lisa James, and thanks."

She smiled and said, "I'm going to be stationed at Fort Bliss, if you ever get out that way." She waived then picked up her bags. The driver shut the door and we headed to the airport.

I caught a shuttle flight to Dallas, Fort Worth so I could catch a direct flight to D.C. After dinner at the airport, I boarded my flight, cuffed my briefcase on the floor to my seat and slept all the way to Washington. I checked the flight schedule and booked myself on a flight to Brussels the following day at three in the afternoon, then got a hotel room. That night at the hotel bar I was having a drink when a very attractive woman took the seat beside me and started up a conversation. I did buy her a drink, and it didn't take long to realize that she was not only friendly but also not the kind of expense that *Mother* would approve, so I finished my drink and went up to my room, alone.

The next morning I went over to the airport and checked-in my bag then caught a taxi to the Pentagon. I stopped at the security desk at the main entrance and showed my credentials and informed the federal police officer that I was armed and he called for an escort to take me to E104. I waited in a small outer office while the Admiral was on the phone. The secretary finally told me I could go in. The Admiral was at his office safe he turned around and handed me the control document to sign, he kept a copy then handed me the document and the letter size package, sealed and stamped CLASSIFIED TOP SECRET, EYES ONLY, for Air Marshal Ari Seversen, Deputy Commander, NATO. I unlocked my briefcase, put the package inside, locked it back then cuffed the case to my left wrist. Back in the outer office I asked the secretary about an FTS line and she pointed to one of the phones on her desk. I picked up the phone and dialed "0" gave the operator my authorization code and the number.

The phone answered and I said. "Redbird, DC, Charlie Alpha." The voice that repeated it back to me was Sergeant Kersie. I told the officer that escorted me and was waiting out side the door that I needed transportation to the airport. He called in on his radio, then took me to the GSA garage and a driver took me to the airport.

I was early so I went ahead and had lunch and killed another hour looking around the shops then went to the boarding area, as per protocol I showed the boarding agent my Courier credentials and my Diplomatic Passport and informed her that I was armed and to inform the Captain. I took my boarding pass and had a seat. Prior to boarding the senior flight attendant came down the ramp and called my name.

"Mr. Whitley I don't have any empty rows so I'm going to put you in First Class, there is plenty of room there, I know you guys prefer not to have people sitting next to you if possible." She said as she smiled and lead me up the ramp into plane.

Of course, the Defense Department doesn't pay for First Class tickets, but one of the other couriers told me they often get upgraded, especially the ones on regular runs. As per airline regulations I uncuffed the case from my wrist placed it on the floor and cuffed it to the under side of my seat then slid it out so I could rest my foot on it.

The in-flight movie was, of all things, *Cabaret* again. The outfit that made that movie must have made a fortune selling it to the airlines. I asked the flight attendant not to wake me for the meal and I got in a couple two to three hour naps. When the plane landed, I was met by a Belgian customs supervisor and he took me through a special gate and stamped my passport. I retrieved by bag and took a taxi to NATO Headquarters.

When I arrived at the Deputy Commander's office he signed for the package, looked at me strangely then asked me my name. He then asked me to wait for a couple of minutes in his outer office while he examined the documents. I asked the secretary if she had a telephone I could call West Germany on and she gave me directions to the communications room. While waiting for the Deputy Commander to give me the OK to leave two other men came in and went into the Air Marshal's private office. The intercom bussed and the secretary answered it, then the voice said. "Tell Mr. Whitley he can leave now." I left the office and followed the secretary's directions to the communications room. When I first walked in to the communications room, the man at the counter started speaking to me in what sounded like German. He acted like he knew me but when I told him I needed a line to West Germany he apologized and directed me to booth number one. I called in and said, "Redbird, Bosco, Tango."

CHAPTER 6.

San Diego

The NATO Deputy Commander's office.

"Well, what do you think?" The Deputy Commander asked Ian MacNally and Eric Goldman generally.

"Absolutely remarkable." Goldman replied.

"Except for the hair color he could be Van Norge's twin brother." Who is he again?" MacNally asked.

"His name is Whitley and he is an American Armed Forces Courier out of Bonn."

"Absolutely remarkable." Goldman repeated himself then continued. Is he military or a civilian, and can we get our hands on him if need be?"

"If he is a military man, favors could be called in without too many questions, but if he is civilian, employee, probably not without bringing the CIA in on the operation."

"If you don't mind my saying so, we are getting ahead of ourselves here. There is no need to bring the Americans in on this, unless it is absolutely necessary." MacNally stated.

"I agree, but, Günter Schmitt should be apprized of this development, just in case. You never know, in an operation like this things have a tendency to change on a moments notice." Colonel Goldman added.

"Good we all agree then, no action at this time, except a discreet inquiry through back channels, on Ian's part, as to the status of this gentleman, and of course, Eric making Günter aware of a potential asset." The Deputy Commander stood up, to let Colonel Eric Goldman and Ian MacNally know that this impromptu meeting was over.

The train ride through Frankfurt to Bonn was restful and I dozed off a couple of times, it's hard not to with the *click clack click clack* of the train on the tracks, but I still needed a good nights sleep.

"Guten Abend Herr Whitley" The desk clerk said as I stopped to pick up my room key.

"Gute Nacht Herr Bauman. I replied as I took my key and headed up the stairs to the second floor.

I unpacked my bag and set aside the stuff that needed to go to the cleaners then called the night duty officer and informed him that I was back, then put on my bathrobe and headed to the shower. When I got back to the room the phone was ringing, it was the duty officer I had just talked to. He said he forgot to tell me that Mother wanted to see me in the morning. Well that was tomorrow, right now nothing is going to stand between me and that soft saggy bed.

The next morning I went down and banged on Ernie's door.

"Hey man. Where have you been, Eddy has been asking about you because Anna is in town?"

"Oh, you know. On the road, here there and

everywhere. Let's go down and get some coffee and catch up. I've got to go see Mother in a couple of hours."

"Yeah, sounds good, I'm off today anyway."

Ernie's biggest gripe was about a new guy in the radio room that just wasn't cutting it, but until one of the older guys with more seniority has to work behind him, it is pointless for Ernie to say anything. Ernie and Eddy had a little spat the other day but they have made up. When I asked him what it was about he said. "You know how girls are, they just get in those moods about once a month when nothing pleases them or is good enough for them, and all they want to do is pick a fight." Well I didn't know first hand, but I agreed with him anyway. School is out for a while and Anna has been bugging Eddy about me, and in turn Eddy has been bugging Ernie, so he asked me if I was going to be around for a while. I told him that I didn't know, but I might be able to do something this afternoon if he can get a hold of the girls.

I went through the vehicle gate instead of going through the building, and walked around the drive to the office and locked my briefcase and revolver in my locker.

"Well Whitley, General Camber's office called and according to Mrs. Camber, quote, *"She couldn't have been in better hands."* Is there something you want to tell me son?"

"She did get away from us at the airport hotel for about 30 minutes and I did have her handcuffed for about 10 minutes at the airport."

"Yeah, I know, the Airport Police made an incident report to our headquarters in Washington, and I got a call yesterday. I just wanted to see if you'd tell me about it. She must have left that part out when she called her husband because they said to commend you on doing a good job."

"Have you got anything else for me?"

"Yep, I've got another job just for you, since you are so good at this escort stuff, but go ahead and get your travel reports caught up, then I'll tell you about it."

While I was doing my travel and expense report, Sergeant Kersie came in.

"Hey Whitley, what's this *"good hands"* stuff. Are you in the insurance business or did you bang that old lady?" Kersie said ribbing me.

I didn't answer her, I just looked up at her for a moment and smiled, then went back to my reports. Kersie tries hard to be just one of the boys, and I don't know for sure, but I don't think it is that much of a stretch.

"Here's the new key card for your scrambler, sign here, and sign the back of the card before you put it in and give me the old one. The keys change at 1600 hours today."

While I was changing the card out in my scrambler she threw a box of ammo on the table and said. "You got a Smith or a Colt?"

"A five shot Colt." I said as I opened the box and looked at the strange ammunition. "What's this?"

"New directive, all couriers are suppose to keep their weapons loaded with these new plastic bullets, you can carry regular ammo for back-up, but keep your piece loaded with these."

"Plastic?"

"Don't let the plastic fool you. We took them over to the gun range, and at close range, there is not much difference, except these things splinter on contact after they have been fired. It has something to do with new airline regulations."

"You done?" Novak asked.

"Yes sir." I said and handed him my reports.

"How's your *per diem*?"

"Right on the money."

"Good, keep it that way. I got a letter from headquarters about some couriers drawing too much advance pay. What about your Government credit card?"

"I know, just transportation expenses, tickets, rental cars and gas, accommodations only in an emergency."

"Good, good. Well since you are all up-to-date and are so good at escort duty, I have another job for you."

"What's that?"

"Since you got along so well with a married 40 year old, how would you like to try a couple of 12 year old girls?"

"Two twelve year old girls?

"We are doing a favor for the Ambassador and you are going to be traveling on the way back at his expense. The twin girls are the Ambassador's nieces and their father is a Federal District Judge, the girls are coming here for a visit then going to a private school in Switzerland. Don't worry Mrs. Posey is going to be with you on the way back."

"Well let me ask a question. If Mrs. Posey is going and they want an armed escort, then why don't they send Sergeant Posey?"

Mr. Novak looked over at Kersie and smiled.

"Yeah, he's sharp alright." She said as she took a dollar out of her pocket and handed it to Novak.

"Well, that was the idea, but the Marine Corps had other plans. Staff Sergeant Posey left yesterday headed for Spain, he's going on a four month Med Cruise with the Fleet Marines. And you, son, are going to San Diego anyway. You leave tomorrow night headed to the Naval Submarine Headquarters in New London, Connecticut and pick up a dispatch going to Hawaii you'll transfer the dispatch to a courier from the Southern California station who'll take it on to Hawaii. Then you hook up with Mrs. Posey and the girls and fly back. Questions?"

"Where do I make the drop off?"

"The Federal Building in San Diego at the office. You'll have plenty of time, you meet Mrs. Posey and the girls at the San Diego airport at 1800 hours Wednesday, she'll have the tickets. You will be taking the night flight to New York, then to London where you catch a flight to Frankfurt then train back here. And Whitley, please don't loose these kids." Novak said and Kersie started laughing behind me.

"Well, I'll see you guys tomorrow afternoon."

I caught up with Ernie and we met the girls at the Bahnhof and took a train to a small farming village on the outskirts of Bonn. We had been invited to dinner at Eddy's grandparents home. Her grandfather with the help of one of her aunt's husband worked the small dairy farm. Eddy's mother had passed away when she was younger and had been raised by her grandparents, her father also lived on the farm but worked in a factory in Bonn. It was kind of a family reunion and there was about fifteen or so people there, not counting us four. Eddy's father as well as most of the younger people there all spoke English to some degree. The girls helped with the food preparation and the grandfather took Ernie, me and another German guy in his twenties, that was engaged to one of the other girls, on a tour of the farm.

Everyone was wonderful to us and treated us like we were part of the family. There were kids of all ages running around and playing with the farm dogs and goats. I talked a long time with Eddy's father and he told me he had been a Sergeant in the German Air Force during the war and had been captured in North Africa and spent three years in Scotland before being returned to Germany. He told me that some of the German prisoners had chosen to stay in Scotland but he wanted to come home to his family. I got the impression that the family had high hopes for Ernie and Eddy and expected an announcement in the near future. Anna and I finally got a chance to spend some time together during dinner, we ate with some of the kids on the back porch. One of the little girls, about six years old had really taken a liking to me and wanted to eat sitting on my lap, and Anna got a real kick out of that and said she could tell I liked kids. I kind of chuckled to myself considering my next assignment.

The food was good home cooking and everyone had a wonderful time. Except for the language, I could have been on a small family farm at a family gathering anywhere in the United States.

We took the train back to the city and walked

to a little bier stub, and Anna wanted to hold my hand while we were walking, which was different because usually the girls walked in front of Ernie and me holding hands with each other. I do believe that Ernie and Eddy are in love and Anna wanted to know what plans I had for tomorrow. She seemed really disappointed when I told her that I would be out of town for a few days.

The next afternoon I checked into the office to go get my briefcase and gun. Mother wasn't at his desk and I checked the board to get my job codes while Kersie was at the back desk on the phone. The first job was Red Fox then I didn't know whether to laugh or not because the job on the way back was Babysitter. Kersie waved as I left the office.

It didn't take long for me to learn how to pack light, just a suit and extra shirt, socks and underwear in my fold-over bag and as long as there was room, my shaving kit in my briefcase. I was becoming a familiar sight on the train to Frankfurt, and would nod or say hello to some of the regular commuters and the train staff. I caught the overnight flight to New York, got some breakfast then took a regional flight to New London.

They wouldn't let the taxi past the gate at the Sub Base, so I had the driver wait and left my bag and told him I would be back in twenty minutes. I told the MP at the gate not to let him leave and the gate supervisor drove me to headquarters. I signed for the dispatch, and checked in on the FTS line then was driven back to the main gate. Back at the regional airport I settled with the cab driver and went in to check on flight schedules. I had a two hour wait for a flight to New York, but I wasn't in a hurry my flight to San Diego wasn't for another six hours. The flight turned out to be a milk run and we made four stops before arriving back in New York.

It was late when I arrived in San Diego so I got a hotel room at the airport.

DeGaul International Airport, France

One of Günter Schmitt's men, Felix, following a Turkish diplomat arrives on a flight, while another one, Borg, has followed Squadron Commander Heiden to the airport. Felix loses the diplomat as he goes through a special line at customs, after he gets through French customs himself, he tries to reacquire the diplomat and when he does he realizes that he is not the only one following him. Felix drops back and follows the unknown man following the diplomat. With both of them in sight now he is joined momentarily by Borg who informs him that Heiden has stopped at an airport kiosk, ordered a beer, and sat down a large bag with a newspaper stuck in the handle, he then continues to walk by Felix. The diplomat stops at the same kiosk and sits his bag and briefcase down at a table next to Heiden and orders a coffee.

Felix signals discreetly to Borg to take over the surveillance and goes to call Günter Schmitt to let him know about the man following the diplomat.

The Turkish diplomat drinks about half of his coffee then casually picks up the bag with the newspaper and leaves the bag he was carrying. The unknown man doesn't follow him but stays with the original bag. Heiden picks up the bag the Turk left behind and heads for the boarding gates. When he stops at the boarding area for a flight going to London, the man following him then hurries to the ticketing area, presumably to buy a ticket for the flight. Borg thinks it is strange that they would have the diplomat bring the bag in through customs then take a regular flight back out of the country. Borg goes to find Felix and tell him of the situation then they both went to buy tickets for the London flight. When Borg and Felix arrive at the boarding gate with their tickets, the unknown man is there looking around and waiting for the flight but there is no sign of Heiden.

The next morning I cleaned up, checked out of the hotel and headed down town to the Federal office building, to drop off my dispatch. I had to wait for about an hour at the field office because they hadn't expected me so early and the other courier wasn't there yet. When the courier arrived I made the transfer, then called in.

"Red Fox Bosco" I said into the phone, it was Sergeant Kersie on the other end.

"Red Fox Bosco" She repeated back to me then said. "You be extra careful with you know who."

"Why, what's up?"

"Well, word has gotten around, and you know how those married women like men with *good hands*." She started laughing then hung up the phone.

Yeah, Ha Ha, I thought to myself and

wondered how long it was going to take for her to get tired of that joke.

I had time to kill so I said to the station chief. "I don't have to be back at the airport until six. What can I do around town here for about four or five hours?"

"I always like going to the zoo when I have spare time." The woman in the office, that was doing some filing, spoke up.

"Yeah, that's a good way to kill a few hours, and you can catch the zoo bus right on the corner." The station chief said.

"That's right, the San Diego Zoo, sometimes I forget what city I'm in. I think that's just the thing. You don't mind if I use one of your lock boxes, do you?"

"Help your self." The station chief said.

I took my Colt out of its holster and placed it in one of the bus station style lockers along with my briefcase and passport then pulled out the key. I took my tie off and hung it on the coat rack in the corner.

The bus was just pulling in when I got outside so I ran to the corner and got on the bus.

"This *is* the zoo bus?" I asked before dropping the change into the box by the driver.

It was only a five minute ride and I could have walked if I had known it was so close. At the zoo I was in line behind a gal with three small kids, carrying two and one by her side.

When she got to the gate she turned around and said. "Can you hold this one?", as she tilted the kid in her right arm toward me. Then reached into her bag for her zoo pass. "Two, three and a stroller." She said to the cashier and the woman punched up two adult and three kids tickets and handed her a large token.

She turned to look at me over her shoulder and said. "Family pass." Without offering to take back the little boy she handed me.

She used the token and pulled a stroller out of the long rack, put the little girl she was holding in one side and took the little boy from me and put him in the other side.

"Thanks for your help. These three can be a hand full sometimes." She said with an British accent.

"Thank you for letting me in with your pass."

"Oh, that. No problem, the Judge and Linda are big supporters of the zoo. We come here at least once a week and sometimes twice. Today we are going to see the Chimp show at the primate pavilion. Have you seen it yet?"

"No, I'm just in town for the day, I've got a flight out at six."

"Aimee, ask him to go with us." The eight year old girl said as she took my hand."

"Sure, I'm Aimee by the way, you want to come see the show with us?"

"I'm Ron and yeah, sounds good to me. So these aren't your kids." We started walking, with Aimee pushing the stroller and the older girl still holding my hand.

"I work for the Fairchilds, you know, to help out with the children, there is another set of twins at home. I'm from England in case you can't tell."

"Does Judge Fairchild have a brother that is the Ambassador to West Germany?"

"Yes." Aimee said as she stopped the stroller

and looked at me with a puzzled expression.

"And the twins are twelve year old girls and are flying to Europe this afternoon."

"What is this. Who are you and what is this all about?" Aimee was getting scared and nervous.

"Relax, I didn't mean to scare you. I'm the escort, I'm taking the twins to Germany."

"You're not the escort, she stayed at the house last night. Who are you, I'm going to call for security."

"Please, I promise you, I know Claire Posey, she works at the Embassy, and I work there too. I'm going to meet them at the airport and go with them." I told her but I still don't think she was convinced. "Here let me show you." I reached for my credentials then realized they were in the locker with my passport, so I went to take out my wallet and she saw the top of my holster and started screaming.

A uniformed security officer came running up to us, by this time the kids are all crying and it's becoming quite a scene. Another officer arrived and they took all of us to the office. I had to explain why I was wearing an empty holster and they took my military ID card and called the courier office at the Federal building.

"He's who he says he is ma'am. Do you want to call home?" Asked the older of the two security officers.

"Did you follow us here?"

"No, I swear, I took the bus from the office to the zoo, I had no idea who you were until we started talking and just put two and two together. I'm sorry, I didn't mean to scare you"

"No, I'm sorry, I got scared when I thought you

had a gun, there have been some threats against the family."

"Can he still come with us to see the monkeys" The girl asked.

"Yes, of course, if he still wants to. I'm sorry I over reacted."

"Are we done here then, Miss Baker." Asked the other security officer.

"Yes, thank you officers, I didn't mean to be so much trouble. Well come on, lets go see the chimpanzees "

We walked and talked some more on the way to the primate pavilion. I asked her if the threats were the reason the girls were going to Europe. She told me no, that the girls were going to go to a private school for girls in Switzerland. The threats were because of a case the Judge is presiding over. The case involves some high ranking gangsters from Long Beach. I knew better than to bring up the fact that at least one of them was probably my step father's brother. Anyway, we watched the Chimp show then walked around looking at the other animals, and the eight year old was holding my hand again. We stopped to get the kids some ice cream and Aimee and I got something to drink.

It turned out to be a pleasant afternoon, even though it got off to a pretty wild start. After we got the kids loaded up in the car, Aimee offered me a ride back to the Federal building. I knew it was pointless to ask her not to tell the Fairchilds about the incident because the little girl wouldn't hesitate to tell all about the excitement that happened. I got out of the car, said good-bye and waived as Aimee pulled away.

The station chief was waiting for me when I got upstairs and wanted to know why the police had called to verify my identity. He listened to my story in disbelief, then said. "Hell of a coincidence, don't you think. You know we are suppose to maintain a low profile. I should send in a incident report, but I won't unless I get something in writing. from the family or the Police."

"Thanks." I said. At least he didn't know how much of a coincidence it was, with my Uncle Paul probably being involved in the case that Judge Fairchild was presiding over. I told him I was going to get an early dinner then head to the airport, and asked him about a place to eat. He told me that if I liked Mexican there was a place called "El Rancho" right behind the Federal building where they sometimes eat. Then said. "Hold on and I'll go with you. Margie, I'll be back in about forty five minutes."

Meanwhile in a NATO briefing room in Belgium. In the room is Günter Schmitt, Ian MacNally and Eric Goldman.

Günter spreads a small stack of photographs on the table and starts to go through them one by one.

"Heiden at the airport in Paris. Acath Agaranik, Turkish Diplomat, arriving at the airport notice the large bag. Heiden and Agaranik sitting next to each other, but not together. The Turk getting up and taking the bag with the newspaper, then leaves his bag behind. This is the man that followed the

Turk off the plane, then followed Heiden after the bag was switched."

"Any idea who he is." Asked Goldman.

"No, he may just be some of Valerian's mussel keeping an eye on the switch. I would like to show his picture to my contact at INTERPOL to see if they can identify him."

"No, No, wait. I don't know who he is but look at this man in the background, and again in this one here. That is Raul something or other, I know him, he is a French policeman." MacNally said as he looked through more photographs. What are these?"

"Similar exchanges, these two in Spain, this man is another Turk, and this one is an American Naval Officer, a Warrant Officer named Walker. These two, right here in Brussels, Van Norge and another Turkish diplomat, and no report of anyone else shadowing the Turks?"

"When are you going to make the proposition to Heiden?" Goldman asked.

"In two more days, then I will let him think about it for a night."

"What about the mysterious meeting you were telling us about." Goldman asked again.

"The meeting is tomorrow night at the Salvagany Hotel in Frankfurt. Maybe our mystery man will be there, but in any case the meeting is with the Russians and not the Turks..

"OK, keep us informed and stay away from INTERPOL and keep an eye out for anyone else doing surveillance.

CHAPTER 7.

Twins and More Twins

Later on that afternoon, I arrived at the departure terminal of the airport and had Claire Posey paged at the information desk. She answered the white courtesy phone and told me that they were at gate twelve. When I found them the DSS resident agent that was with them said. "They're all yours." and left.

"Well, Whitley, I hear you had an exciting day."

"Yeah, I met Aimee and the other kids."

"So we were told, anyway, this is Casey and Lacy. Girls this is Mister Whitley, he is going to go with us to Germany."

"Hello ladies."

"Pleased to meet you, Mister Whitley, I'm Casey." She smiled and did a little curtsy.

"And I am Lacy, Aimee said you were cute." Lacy said as she extended her hand for me to shake, like a proper well breed young lady.

The girls were well mannered and absolutely adorable.

"Claire, can we get a snack before the flight, we're hungry. Lacy asked. She was obviously the more precocious of the two.

"I don't see why not, we have plenty of time

and Mister Whitley needs to check-in." Claire said as she handed me the tickets, boarding passes and passports.

I walked with the ladies to the café at the beginning of the gate area. The girls wanted french-fries and cokes, Claire just wanted coffee. When the order was ready I dropped it off at the table then went to check-in, showed my credentials as well as my passport and informed them that I was armed, as required. The supervisor came out and asked me if I was aware of the new requirements for carrying in-flight firearms. I told her I was, and had the new ammunition. She said that the Captain might want to check for himself and I told her that was no problem and she gave me the boarding passes.

When I returned to the café Lacy had finished her french-fries and Casey was just picking at hers. I sat down and drank my coffee. Lacy was just full of questions and asked me if I thought Aimee was beautiful. I told her I did.

"Oh, I almost forgot." Claire said and opened her handbag and took out a letter for me.

The letter was from Aimee, it didn't say much except that if I got back to San Diego, I should call her and she included a phone number. I put the letter away, with out really thinking much about it. Our tickets were for first class and both girls wanted to sit by the window, so Casey sat with Claire and Lacy sat with me in the row behind. We had a two hour lay over in New York before the flight to London. I took the opportunity to call in then verified that the girls' bags were checked through. Lacy was hungry again so we got something to eat, but Casey just wanted a 7Up. Claire tried go get her to eat something but she just wasn't having it.

About three hours into the flight both the girls were asleep. Claire turned around in her seat and asked me if Lacy was hot. I checked Lacy she was sound asleep and drooling a little but she felt cool to me so I took the little blanket and covered her up. Claire turned around again and said that Casey was burning up. I got out of my seat to check she did have a little fever, but I also noticed that the air vent for her seat wasn't turned on, so I reached up and turned the knob to open the vent fully. We agreed to just let her sleep for now and take her temperature when she woke up. By this time the flight attendant was there and felt her head, and said she would get a thermometer and a damp towel to put on her forehead.

Four hours into the flight Casey woke up with severe stomach cramps, and her temperature was 102. The flight attendant said there was a Doctor on the manifest and she would wake him. It turned out he was a College Professor and not a physician but the lady across the aisle over heard and was a Registered Nurse. The nurse said we had to try and bring her fever down and after a quick examination the nurse said that she thought the child had appendicitis. The flight attendant went to let the Captain know what was going on. A couple of minutes later the Captain came back and looked at Casey and talked with the nurse. He said we were past the point of no return and it would be faster to continue on to London and he would call ahead for an ambulance. I explained to the Captain who the girls were and told him I needed to get a message through to the Embassy. He told me to write it out and give it to the flight attendant. I figured I had better go through the office with the message and started with the phone number to the duty phone. When I finished the message read.

URGENT
CONTACT EAGLE
ONE DUCKLING ILL
REQUIRES HOSPITAL LONDON
HAVE LONDON PERCH MEET FLIGHT TWA104
ARRIVE LONDON TIME 1545
SIGNED BABYSITTER.

I gave the paper to the flight attendant and told her to have London call the number indicated in West Germany and read the message exactly as written. She told me the Captain was waiting and would make the call immediately. In the mean time Claire and the nurse moved Casey to an empty row and undressed her and kept wiping her down with cool damp towels.

The flight attendants were doing the dinner service, but I didn't want to wake Lacy, I figured as long as she was sleeping the better off it would be. I walked back to the galley to get a cup of coffee and was handed a note, it read.

TO BABYSITTER
MESSAGE UNDERSTOOD
BIRDIE AND MOTHER DUCK IN ROUTE
LONDON CLAW WILL HANDLE
CONTINUE MISSION WITH ONE DUCKLING
ON FLIGHT BRINGING BIRDIE
SIGNED MOTHER

I showed the note to Claire and she asked.

"What about me?"

"Well since they want Lacy to go on to Bonn on the flight bringing the Ambassador's wife, I assume you will stay with me and Lacy. She will probably be coming in on a special charter or a military flight."

The over head speakers came to life. "LADIES AND GENTLEMEN, THIS IS YOUR CAPTAIN. WE WILL BE LANDING AT HEATHROW AIRPORT IN ABOUT FOURTYFIVE MINUTES. LONDON TIME IS CURRENTLY THREE PM IF YOU WANT TO SET YOUR WATCHES THERE WILL BE A SLIGHT DELAY WHEN WE LAND, WE HAVE A MEDICAL EMERGENCY IN FIRST CLASS THAT WILL NEED TO BE OFF LOADED FIRST. WHEN WE ARE GIVEN THE OK, WE WILL THEN TAXI TO THE ARRIVING CUSTOMS TERMINAL FOR DE-PLANEING. IN ABOUT TWENTY MINUTES THE FLIGHT ATTENDANTS WILL BE GIVING YOU LANDING INSTRUCTIONS. THANK YOU FOR FLYING TWA."

"How are you doing Casey?" I said as I knelt down and held her hand.

"My tummy hurts."

"I know it does baby, just hang in there a little while longer, there will be a Doctor as soon as we land, and he will make you feel better."

"What's wrong with Casey?" Lacy asked with tears in her eyes. She had been awakened by the Captain's announcement and came looking for us.

Claire put her arm around Lacy to comfort her and said. "She is sick but we are taking care of her and she is going to be fine."

Lacy pulled away from Claire and put her arm around my neck with tears starting to streak her face. These two are definitely Daddy's girls.

"There's no reason to cry sweetie, she is going

to be OK. Do you want to sit here on the floor and hold Casey's hand for a while?"

"Yes please. Are you going to stay with us?"

"Of course, Mrs. Posey and I are going to stay with you. When your Aunt arrives, she is going to stay with Casey and we are going on to Germany. In a couple of days when Casey is better your Aunt will bring her too."

I got up and left Claire and the nurse with the girls, and went to the galley to get that cup of coffee I started to get earlier. The flight attendants were just about finished cleaning up after dinner and I stayed in the galley area drinking my coffee. About ten minutes later the Senior Flight Attendant got on the intercom and advised everyone to return to their seats and the other attendants started to go over the landing procedures. Claire sat in the row with Casey and put her head in her lap while she was being buckled up by one of the attendants. I took Lacy and went back to our seats and buckled up.

After we landed and were slowing down we could see out the window several vehicles with flashing lights coming out to meet us. A portable stair was driven up to the forward cabin door and a Doctor, two ambulance attendants, two DSS Agents and a British Customs Official came aboard. While the Doctor was examining Casey I gave all four passports to the Customs Official, Claire and I both had diplomatic passports, and I told him that the three of us would be continuing on to Germany. He asked which of the girls was which. I told him and he handed Casey's passport to one of the DSS Agents and gave the other three back to me.

"Roger, understand." The second DSS Agent

spoke into his radio then turned to us and said. The C130 with the Ambassador's wife has landed and they are bringing her here to us."

The ambulance attendants had Casey on a stretcher and were heading to the door with the Doctor following. I got my briefcase and bag out of the over head while Claire got hers and the two girls carry on bags. Lacy stayed by my side and we followed everyone off the plane. While Casey was being loaded into the ambulance another lemo pulled up with the Ambassador's wife and a DSS Agent from Bonn. She came running over to us and bent over and hugged and kissed Lacy and said. "I love you darling, your Uncle and your Cousin Carla are waiting to see you. I am going to the hospital with your sister and we'll be home in a few days."

"Excuse me ma'am, the ambulance is ready to go, and this is Agent Stokes, he'll be taking over from me."

"Thank you, Bill, and thank you both for taking care of my nieces. I love you darling and I'll see you in a few days, and your mother is on her way over." With that, Agent Stokes took her by the arm and helped her into the waiting ambulance, then followed them in a lemo.

Agent Bill Folks then turned to us and said. "You guys are with me." Then spoke into his radio. "Travelers are on the way."

We were driven to the waiting C130 and in a few minutes we were on our way. After landing in Frankfurt we were transferred to a waiting helicopter and flew to Bonn and landed at the Embassy in the grassy area in the center of the circle drive behind the main building.

We got our bags and moved over to the drive then the helicopter took off, as soon as it cleared the compound the back vehicle gate, that went to the residence, opened and a sedan pulled up

"Let's get the young lady settled then I'll drive you home Mrs. Posey. How about you?" Bill Folks asked.

"No, I'm fine, I have to check in to the office anyway."

Lacy waived and said "Good-bye" as the sedan pulled off. I walked on around the drive to the office and saw one of the Marines locking the gate back after the car pulled through.

I was surprised to find Mr. Novak still in the office, but he was waiting for me. Apparently since my message was called in from London, things have really been hopping around the Embassy.

"I thought you would want to know, I got a call from DSS about five minutes ago. It was appendicitis, the operation is over and she is going to be OK. Are you tired?"

"Yes sir, I am."

"I figured you would be. Lock your stuff up and go home. You can do your paperwork tomorrow afternoon."

"Crap. I've still got Claire and Lacy's passports." I said as I took out their travel documents and the unused portions of the airline tickets and gave them to Novak. Then continued to lock my briefcase and gun up in my locker.

"Oh, and Whitley" Novak said as I headed for the door. I turned to look at him and he continued. "You did good."

The next morning the phone rang way too

early, it was Mr. Novak telling me that the Ambassador wanted to see me and Claire Posey in his office at 1000 hours.

I walked over to the Embassy the next morning with Ernie who was back on the morning shift. We went to the cafeteria and were having breakfast when Peacoe stopped by the table.

"Well Whitley, I understand you've been on quite an adventure."

"Yes sir." I said not really knowing how to take the comment. I could never figure out when Peacoe was playing at being a prick, or just being his natural asshole self.

"I've been doing a little regulation reading and I found out something, you might be interested in this. According to the regulations you have to be at least a Sergeant or a Specialist Five to be assigned to the Armed Forces Courier Service." With that Peacoe continued on and took a seat a couple of tables away.

"What was that all about?" Ernie asked.

"You know, Sergeant Peacoe has been trying to get rid of me ever since I got here. I thought I had him off my ass when I got assigned to the Courier Service, but I guess he still has a burr up his ass."

After breakfast I went up to Mr. Wellborn's office to find Claire and wait for time to see the Ambassador. This was the first time I would actually meet Ambassador Fairchild, of course I have seen him around the Embassy several times but never spoke to him. I knocked on the door then went on in. Claire wasn't at her desk but Mr. Wellborn opened the door to his office.

"Oh, Whitley it's you. Claire will be back in a

couple of minutes, she's just down the hall. Oh, and Whitley, you handled the situation, with the girls, perfectly."

"Thank you, but Mrs. Posey did most of it and we were lucky enough to have a nurse on board."

"That's right, Claire told me all about it, but I'm talking about staying calm and taking charge. You know when your time is up in the Army you might think about the DSS for a career."

The door opened and Claire entered the office. She motioned for me to have a seat and went inside Wellborn's private office and closed the door. She came back out a couple of minutes later without him and took a seat at her desk. We talked for awhile then she got the call for us to go up stairs.

On the way up to the Ambassador's office she told me that Peacoe was causing some kind of stink about something, but Major Bestler was working on it.

Ambassador Fairchild is a very distinguished looking man in his late forties. A lot of the Ambassadors are just political appointees that change with the Presidents, but Fairchild is a career diplomat and was formerly the Consul General to Argentina. There were several people in the office including Major Bestler.

"You both will be receiving personal letters of commendation from me, but I had you come here today to personally thank you for taking such excellent care of my nieces. Claire we are going to miss you around here when Staff Sergeant Posey is reassigned. I've asked that he be retained here to take Gunnery Sergeant Berks' place, but you know how possessive the Marine Corps is about its personnel."

Claire smiled and just said. "Yes Mister Ambassador, I do."

"As for you Mister Whitley, although we couldn't keep you on staff, I'm glad Major Bestler found you a job with the Courier Service. I will be sending you a letter of recommendation to the State Department in case you want to apply for a position if you decide not to stay in the Army. We will be having a birthday party for the twins when Casey arrives. I hope you both will be able to attend."

"Thank you sir."

"I'm sorry I have to cut this short, but I have another meeting. Again thank you both for your excellent service."

After we left the office, Major Bestler told me to check in with Mr. Novak, because he had some news for me. I walked over to our building and entered the office.

"Good, you're here, before you start your paper work, I've got something I have to tell you." Mr. Novak said as he barely looked up from his desk, then continued. "It seems your buddy Peacoe has been sticking his nose in where it doesn't belong. He managed to get a copy of your waiver sent to him and was kind enough to point out that the waiver only covers your age, and not your rank."

"Am I in trouble?"

"No, but it seems that I am. You know Whitley, you've done a good job in the short time you have been here, and I don't really have a choice in the matter."

"I'm going to be reassigned. I mean, that is what you're talking about, isn't it?"

"Well yes. I received this message from

Headquarters, and it concerns you. Why don't you read it for your self." Novak handed me the message without looking up.

I took the message and read it, then looked at Mr. Novak.

"That's right. We only had two choices, reassign you or promote you. So effective today, you are promoted to Specialist Five, signed by the Commander of the Armed Forces Courier Service. So congratulations and you better get started on that paper work. Oh and Whitley, I'll inform Master Sergeant Peacoe myself, we don't want him wasting any more time worrying about your welfare. Now do we?"

CHAPTER 8.

The Birthday Party

The Salvagny Hotel in Frankfurt.

Günter Schmitt arrives at the hotel early the day of the meeting and two hundred Marks in the right pocket, he gets a look at the reservations. There was only five to choose from, and only one Russian, so he figured that was it and asked if there was an adjoining room, then told the desk clerk that was the one he wanted. Günter carried his own bag up to the room, then another hundred Marks in the pocket of the maid on the floor and she unlocked the door to the adjoining room. As soon as the maid left the room Günter opened his case and got busy. There was two doors between the rooms, and with both doors open, he gets out a spool of wire, a razor knife, and two pieces of a metal rod and screws them together. Starting in his room he takes the razor knife and cuts a small slit in the carpet then attaches the wire to one end of the rod and pushes it under the carpet. He then finds the end of the rod and makes another small slit and pulls the rod thru then reinserts it in the same slit and repeats the process, like a needle pulling thread.

He runs one set of wires to behind the dresser, and another set across the room to behind the night stand, and yet another to the telephone jack. He attaches round flat microphones to the ends of the wires and the other ends he attaches to the tape recorder he sat on the dresser in his room. After he connects to the phone jack and hides the wire underneath the original wire and connects the other end to a special telephone recorder that turns on when the hand set is picked up. The next step he takes a small transistor radio, places it in the center of the room with the volume down low, goes back to his room and plugs in the earphones and adjusts the gain inputs on the recorder.

Everything set, he retrieves the radio and locks the adjoining door from inside the room then exits out the door to the hall, and as soon as he shuts the door, he realizes that he doesn't have the key to his room. After finding the maid he slips her another ten marks to open the door to his room. He locks the other adjoining door from his side, and figures the maid will be nosiy and try to find out what he was doing in the other room. He sits down in front of the dresser and puts the earphones in and listens. He was right, he hears the door open and the maid checking the drawers in the dresser he hears her moving around in the room, then leaves. The final test he thought, if the maid couldn't find any thing out of place then he was safe. Now to just sit back and relax for a few hours and wait for the meeting.

Office of Inspector DeLeon, head of the anti drug division of the French National Police, Paris.

Inspector DeLeon introduces Deputy Chief Inspector Franklin from Scotland Yard to his team working a major drug case. During their investigation, they have run into an individual, possibly an Irish or English citizen they are trying to identify. The police are not sure what he has to do with the drug ring, but he keeps turning up in the investigation. DCI Franklin knows the subject is Sean O'Finn, an IRA bomber and *hit man* wanted in England and Northern Ireland, for murder, but he is not going to share that information with the French. His mission is to gather and relay as much information on O'Finn's location and activities as he can. Inspector DeLeon, however, believes DCI Franklin is there to be a liaison between them and Scotland Yard, and to help identify their mystery man.

Inspector DeLeon's team of investigators have identified the opium as being Turkish and believe it is being brought in by either Turkish airline personnel or Turkish Diplomats, but they haven't yet identified the couriers, but are close to doing so.

Back in Bonn.

I just returned from a job, Spain to Iceland, to the Pentagon, and back to Spain, and as usual I am tired and need to catch up on my sleep. I stopped by the front desk to pick up my room key, and my dry cleaning and laundry. Good, I said to myself on the way up to my room, my dress whites are back from the drycleaners, the ones I had been issued by the clothing sales store in Frankfurt. Of course I never dreamed I would be making Spec Five so fast or I would have had the patches sewn on. Anyway I'm glad their back, the birthday party at the residence is tomorrow night.

Normally someone of my rank would never be invited to any kind of function at the residence, except for the mandatory New Year's Day brunch with the Ambassador and his family that all the military personnel attend.

I called the office and informed *Mother* that I was back and told him I would be in first thing in the morning to do my paper work. I had an early dinner in the hotel dinning room, then decided to turn in.

Back at the Salvagny Hotel, in Frankfurt.

Günter Schmitt covers the tape recorders on the dresser with his over coat then opens the door to let the room service porter in with his dinner. He holds on to the door with his right hand and motions with his left. "Das ist gut, danke." Günter says, indicating to the porter to just leave the dinner cart inside the door. The porter pushes the cart inside the room then takes the tip from Günter's hand then bows slightly and backs out of the room closing the door. Günter latches the privacy lock on the door then pushes the cart over to the dresser where he has his chair. About half way through dinner, he hears some voices in the distance, then he hears the door to the other room open. He turns down the speaker and starts the recorder.

There is two of them in the room, and they are speaking Russian. Günter only understands a small part of what they are talking about, but enough to know he has the right room and one of the voices sounds like the old fart Colonel Valerie Valerian himself.

The telephone rings in the room, the second Russian, Mikiel, answers the call, it is the desk clerk announcing Herr Heiden and Herr Van Norge. He tells him it is OK to send them up. Günter had already called in to the phone drop with his room number so either Borg or Felix should be knocking on the door shortly.

About a minute after Heiden and Van Norge arrive in the Russian's room, there is a light tap at the door, it is Felix. He tells Günter that there is something wrong. Heiden and Van Norge came in together on the train from Brussels and argued several times during the trip.

"Could you tell what the argument was about?"

"Couldn't get close enough to hear, but it seemed like Heiden was really *on the cheek* about something, it was almost like he was pleading with Van Norge." Felix replied.

"Where is Borg?"

"In front of the hotel, the lobby would be too obvious."

"They came together, so they will probably leave together. Let Borg stay on the Dutchmen, you take my auto keys and wait for the Russians. I think Valerian is in the next room, if they split up, stay on him, if not take your choice."

"Where is the auto?" Felix asked as he picked up the keys and put them in his coat pocket, then got a brotchen and a piece of cheese from Günter's plate. "In the parking lot, and get your own food."

The next morning I had breakfast at the Embassy cafeteria then went over to the office to do my paper work. I unlocked my case and got out my logs and receipts, then locked my gun and courier case in my locker. Mr. Novak had looked up when I came into the office but went back to his conversation with Sergeant Kersie. They were trying to decide why Petty Officer Johnson, one of the other military couriers, hasn't called in a *BOSCO* on his last job. If he doesn't call in this morning, they will have to dispatch another courier to the job they have waiting in Italy. When Sergeant Weathers leaves next week, Johnson and I will be the only two military couriers here, the rest of the guys are Department of Defense civilians employees. The only difference, of course, is that they make a hell of a lot more money than we do. I was about half way through my paper work when the duty phone rang. It must have been Johnson because Kersie said. "Hound dog, Bosco, call your Mother. Got him Chief." She called out to Novak as she hung up the phone.

"Good. I'll call Carlos and tell him he can cancel. Whitley when you're done in there I need to talk to you."

"Yes sir." I said wondering what I've done now. I finished up my stuff then went to Novak's desk and put it in his in-box, then just stood there for a moment.

Finally Novak looked up at me, said have a seat

and then asked. "Your time is going to be up in about four months. Have you given any thought about if you are going to stay in the army or get out?"

"Yes sir, sometimes I think about making it a career, and other times I think I want to get out and go to a real college. I guess what I'm saying is, I just don't know yet."

"Well, you are going to have to make up your mind, time is going to run out on you."

"What do you think I should do?"

"I can't tell you what to do, but I will tell you that I started out like you. A buck private, right out of school, you see in the city where I grew up, you either became a cop, a wise guy, or pushed a cart in the produce mart. Of course if you had the money you could go to college, about the only other choice was the military. I joined up, like you, I went to college at night and correspondence, and when I made Staff Sergeant, I put in for Warrant, and now twelve years later, I have a good job, I've seen the world and am looking forward to retirement. But back to you, you are an E5 now and have to have a secondary MOS.

"What's wrong with the one I have?"

"You mean Duty Soldier, well that will change when you leave here anyway, depending on what your new assignment is. No, I'm talking about a secondary MOS, all E5s and above are required to have a secondary job classification now. Regulations, you know."

"Doesn't the army just pick one for me?"

"They will if you don't, but if I were you, I wouldn't leave it up to the Army. There are two ways to go, first is with something you already have some training in, like demolitions, or administration. That way you won't have to study so hard for your examinations when they come up. Your second choice is to pick one off the critical shortage list. Any time a MOS is in shortage, that's where the promotions are. That would be the smart thing to do. Here is what I use to be, a 97C, Area Intelligence Analyst."

"What the heck is that?"

"Well it is part of the Military Intelligence Field, but don't worry about it. It requires training, so if you decide to reenlist, 90 days before you are due to go back to the States, you apply for the school and they will put you on the list. So how about it?"

"OK, let's put it down."

"Good, that part is settled, now all we need to know is what to tell headquarters. If you are not going to reenlist, I need to know, so I can request a replacement, and if you are, headquarters needs to know so they can change you from a 1 year tour to a 3 year tour."

"How long do I have to let you know."

"I think you already know, but you can take a couple of days to think about it. In the mean time get out of here and do something before I send you back out."

Novak was right, I already knew. My only chance of getting a 4 year college degree was to do it a little at a time in the army just like I have been doing. Even with the GI Bill it would be rough on the outside, I would have to work a job and go to school full time, not to mention trying to have some kind of social life. That's not to say that I have one now, being gone over half the time, but I really like my job, and I want to stay, and college is easier because I only have to study one course at a time.

Later on that afternoon I was starting to get ready for the birthday party when Ernie came by the room. He told me that Anna was back in school and kept beating around the bush about something. I could tell he had something on his mind he wanted to talk about, so I finally just asked him straight out.

"I think I'm in love man."

"So what's the problem?"

"I'm mean really in love, like I want to marry the girl?"

"Have you told her, I mean don't you think you should?"

"That's just it. What if I ask her to marry me and she says no. I don't want her to think I'm going too fast. She might not only say no, but she may want to stop seeing me"

"Oh, well, I'm not the one you need to be talking to. I mean I can't give you advice on something like this. I kind of thought you two were perfect for each other."

"I do too, that's why I don't want to take the chance."

"All I can tell you is that Eddy's family seems like they really like you. Why don't you just ask her how she feels and where she wants the relationship to go? Anyway, like I said, I'm not the one to be giving you advice on this, I mean, what the hell do I know?"

"I could just not say anything and see if she brings the subject up. Anyway, thanks, I'll let you finish getting ready." With that Ernie just shook his head and left the room.

I looked sharp in my whites, and headed over

to the Embassy residence. I was right on time when I pushed the button at the foot gate in front of the residence. The Marine inside the little guard house by the front door buzzed me through the gate while another one was checking-in a lemo at the vehicle gate. This was the first time for me going to the residence and I was nervous. I hoped like hell that I wouldn't spill anything on this white uniform.

The place wasn't as fancy as I thought it would be. Don't get me wrong, it was elegant, but really just a big house, and I do mean big. The actual living quarters were on the upper floors, on the first floor there was a coat room just off the foyer where I put my hat on a shelf beside some others. Then through another set of open doors a large reception room, with seating around the perimeter and the largest formal dining room I've have ever seen, the table in the center of the room looked like it could seat 30 people. There were two other open rooms, a library and a room that was called the *Jägerzimmer,* which had a bar, a billiards table, and some fish, boar and deer heads hanging on the walls.

As more and more people arrived, it became apparent to me that this was not just a small birthday party, but more of an ambassadorial function and I really felt out of place. I looked around the room for uniforms. I saw Major Bestler was also wearing dress whites, and was talking with a British Brigadier and his aide. There was also two German officers, one of which I think was a general and another officer in a uniform that I didn't recognize with a rather large woman, presumably his wife.

I was so nervous I damn near jumped out of my skin when someone walked up behind me and put there hand on my back. It was Claire Posey and thank God, someone I can talk to.

"Relax, let's get a drink."

"Hi. I'm glad you're here. Do you know any of these people."

"Oh, some of them are the regulars, they get invited to all the functions, like Prince Sevinski over there."

"Which one is he, I've never seen a prince before?"

"That one over there, the one with the fat wife and watch her, she has been known to corner young men, if you know what I mean. He really is a Polish Prince, but it's just a title, you know, he doesn't do anything. Come on let's go get that drink." She said as I followed her to the room with the bar.

Claire ordered a glass of white wine but I was so afraid that I would spill something on my uniform, I decided not to have anything until after the family came down.

"It sounds like they are getting ready, let's go and get in the reception line." Claire sat her glass down on the bar, and we walked back into the reception room and joined the line.

The Ambassador his wife and daughter, along with Lacy, Casey and who I guessed was their mother, were at the foot of the stairs greeting people. Claire and I joined the line and when it was our turn the Ambassador introduced us to the other Mrs. Fairchild who was absolutely beautiful and hardly looked old enough to be the girls' mother.

"Hi Claire, I know you'll be glad when your husband gets home." The Ambassador's wife said.

"Three more months." Claire said.

"In the mean time, it looks like you have an excellent escort."

"I have been wanting to meet you Mr. Whitley. I want to thank you so much for taking such good care of the girls. They have told me so much about the trip." The gorgeous petite blond said as she held out her hand.

After shaking hands with Mrs. Fairchild, Lacy motioned for me to bend down so she could tell me something. When I did both of the girls took turns hugging me around the neck and kissing me on the cheek, then both of them hugged Claire around the waist. There were still guest behind us so we shook hands with the Ambassador and his wife then moved on. I figured it was time for that drink so I told Claire that I was going back to the bar and get a beer.

I had just ordered a beer when in came Major Bestler and introduced me to Jack Roark, the Assistant Cultural Attaché. There was something about Roark that I can't put my finger on, but he didn't impress me as the diplomat type. If I had to guess I would say he was a military man or ex-military maybe. He didn't have much to say except that he was also from Kentucky and asked if I would stop by his office some time. He then looked away and continued talking with Major Bestler. It was evident that I wasn't included in the conversation so when John one of the Marines dressed in a waiter's uniform handed me the beer I ordered, I asked him if he was on duty or just moonlighting.

"Hang on a second." He said as he made a couple of drinks and handed them to Bestler and Roark then continued. "Both, I'm on duty, but we get paid extra when we work these things. Oh, watch out for the fat broad, she's already been over here twice hitting on me."

"Maybe she's just looking for a *Few Good Men,* John, anyway let me have a glass of white wine while you're at it." I said as I saw Claire heading toward us.

John sat the glass of wine on the bar, then turned to wait on a couple more people.

"Is this for me?"

"Yes Ma'am." I said.

"Hey Mrs. P. Does the Staff Sergeant know you've been hanging around with this no class Army dude?"

"You better just hope I don't tell him you were trying to get me drunk, John." She said and John just smiled and chuckled at her.

"How long am I suppose to stick around this shin-dig, you know, when can I slip out without being rude?"

"You'll need to stay until after they cut the birthday cake. Aren't you having a good time?"

"It's OK I guess, but I do feel a little out of place."

"I know what you mean, me too. They've started eating if you want to get a plate from the buffet."

"Nah, I think I'll pass."

"Well I'm hungry." Claire said as she handed me her now empty glass and headed for the dining room.

Before I finished my beer, in came the twins followed by their mother, man what a good looking woman. The girls wanted to play pool and Lacy asked me to be her partner and play against Casey and mom, but Mrs. Fairchild spoke up.

"Why don't you girls play, I want to talk to Mr. Whitley for a minute. Do you mind Mr. Whitley?"

"Not at all, Ma'am."

"Please, call me Linda. Let's go into the Library where we can sit down." She turned and I followed her out the door and down the short hall to the Library and I could smell that perfume of hers all the way. I had a grade school teacher who wore jasmine perfume, but it didn't smell as good as it does on Mrs. Fairchild.

There was a small group of men standing and sitting in front of the huge fireplace deep in conversation about something or other. We sat at the other end of the room in some chairs grouped around a small table. I was curious as to why she wanted to talk to me, then confused when she started asking me questions like, was I married and what kind of education I had. Then it started to become a little clearer when out of the clear blue she asked me what I thought about Aimee.

"We think of Aimee like another daughter, and she is so naive when it comes to men. And since she couldn't stop talking about you the day you two met. Well, you understand, I was more than a little curious."

"I understand, but I don't really know what to tell you. I just met her, and I think she is nice, but I probably won't get back to San Diego, I normally just travel between Europe and the east coast."

"Well, I must tell you, she is quite taken with you, and now that I've met you, I can see why. She wants to correspond with you, that can't hurt anything. Can it?"

"No, I guess, but I don't know if it will come to anything."

"Good, but in any case, try not to hurt her, she is such a sweet girl, just not very wise to the world." She said as she opened the small handbag she was carrying and handed me a letter from Aimee. "Well, I want to thank you for having this talk with me. You've eased my mind, and if you ever do get to San Diego, you are more than welcome to stay with us. All the kids would love it."

"Thank you very much, Mrs. Fairchild. I said as she stood up and so did I and shuck her hand again as she offered it.

That was all pretty unexpected, especially about a girl I had only spent one afternoon with. Aimee was nice enough and cute as well, but definitely not as hot as momma. I still can't believe Linda Fairchild is old enough to have twelve year old girls not to mention five kids altogether.

It wasn't long before they did the happy birthday thing and cut the big cake. I hung around for about another ten minutes then decided to slip out. I looked for Claire before I left, but didn't see her. I knew she would be fine, she is like the den mother of the marines, so I knew they would take care of her.

CHAPTER 9.

A Temporary Assignment

Paris, Inspector DeLeon's office.

Deputy Chief Inspector Franklin from Scotland Yard, sits in on a meeting about the ongoing drug investigation. One of the French policemen reads three surveillance reports, one of which concerns the mystery man the French are trying to identify. Franklin makes notes of the information, to relay to Sir William.

The next week or so was busy. I had made the NATO Round Robin and a trip to the Pentagon and as soon as I got back I left to pick up a job in Spain going to Italy. There was no pick-up in Italy so I spent the night in a hotel to get some sleep then caught a train and headed back to Germany. It was late when I got back so I called the night duty officer to report in, and was told that Mother wanted to see me. I told him I would see Mr. Novak in the morning when I came in to do my paper work.

I slept in the next morning, it was about 0900 when I got up, I had really come to love that saggy old bed in the hotel. It was about 1015 when I arrived at the office. I wasn't worried about coming in this late because I knew I was due for some down time.

"Good morning." I said as I came in and went to the table in the big room and opened my case to get out the stuff I needed to do my travel report. Novak acted like he didn't hear me but Sergeant Kersie who was on the phone at her desk waived. I put my briefcase and gun in my locker and as soon as I snapped the lock, I heard.

"About time you decided to come to work. You think I'm running a resort here?" Novak said in a gruff voice, but he wasn't mad. He just felt the need to remind us every once in a while who the boss was.

"No Sir, it was just real late when I got in last night."

"I know what time you got in, it's right here in the log. Anyway, what did you decided about re-enlistment?"

"Well after thinking it over, I decided I want to stay in."

"Son-of-a-bitch." Kersie said and got up and walked over to Novak's desk and threw a dollar bill on it, then went back to her desk.

"Good, I thought that is what you would say. I've already got your papers typed up. All you have to do is sign and I'll swear you in."

Well it wasn't much of a ceremony, but at least I don't have to think about it anymore, not for another four years anyway. I finished my paper work then walked over to the communications center to let Ernie know I was back and would be off for a couple of days. He was just getting ready to go to lunch so we walked down to the dining room together.

Belgium, NATO Headquarters, Office of Colonel Eric Goldman. Günter Schmitt is present.

"Say that again." Goldman said with a puzzled look on his face.

"He's dead."

"What do you mean he's dead?"

"Just what I said, he's dead. We talked to Van Norge and Heiden both last night and I laid out their options, 20 years in jail or cooperate with us. I thought we had both of them ready to work for us. Van Norge, however, must have came up with an option of his own."

"Tell me exactly what went down."

"We wanted to confront them before the weekend, so I had Borg and two men pick up Heiden at his home, his wife and children are in Holland on holiday. Felix and two more of my men picked up Van Norge as he was leaving his apartment. Both men were blindfolded and taken to the Brussels safe house. I told them what I had on them, showed them some of the surveillance photographs, told them their military careers were over and both of them faced a minimum of 20 years in a military prison unless they started to work for us. They agreed and we spent the next four hours questioning them about the details of the operation, contacts, time schedules, signals, code words, and names, a lot of names."

"So what went wrong?"

"Nothing, everything went as planned and after

four hours of tape recording the interrogations we re-blindfolded them and took them back to where we picked them up with instructions not to make contact with anyone until we told them to do so. Of course we maintained the surveillance and monitored the phone taps. Van Norge's girlfriend, one of ours, a Miss Mare Van Meter, call around midnight to tell him she would be about an hour late in the morning, she had to run an errand for a girlfriend of hers. They had plans to spend the day together."

"OK, OK, get on with it."

"Well, she arrived this morning about 10 but he didn't answer the door. She stayed for about fifteen minutes knocking on the door and ringing the bell, finally a man who lives in the apartment across the hall opened his door, they had a few words and she left. A few minutes later my men called the apartment, they got no answer so they entered to see if they somehow missed Van Norge."

"Well?"

"They found him in the in the bathroom on the floor with a broken neck, it appears that he slipped getting out of the shower. They then called me. I had Felix go to the apartment in the van. They rolled him up in a rug and carried him out. There was no sign that anyone else had been in the apartment so they collected all his personal papers and identification and took him to a funeral director friend of mine to keep the body on ice until I could talk to you." Günter said as he tossed a large envelope, containing Van Norge's papers in it, down on Eric's desk.

Eric picked up the telephone and dialed a phone number. "Colonel Goldman for Director MacNally." "Hello, Ian. Better come to my office we have a problem here."

I went out to dinner with Ernie and Eddy that evening and they announced their engagement. We celebrated a little too well that evening and I awoke the next morning with one hell of a hang over. I struggled to the bath, hoping that a good shower would help me feel a little better. I spend the day out sightseeing and just relaxing then went to a German movie that evening. The phone was ringing when I returned to my room that night.

"Hello"

"Whitley this is Jack Roark, the Assistant Cultural Attaché, we met at the birthday party."

"Yes Sir, I remember, what can I do for you?"

"Well, I've got a job you might be interested in."

"Yes Sir, I appreciate that, but shouldn't you be talking to Mr. Novak?"

"I've already talked with Jim, let's say you meet me in my office about 1300."

"Yes Sir." I said, but he had already hung up the phone. I tried to figure out what the hell this guy wanted and the only thing I could come up with, was another personal favor for the Ambassador. But since he has already talked with my boss, I guess it wouldn't hurt to go hear what he has to say, besides, he has my curiosity up.

The next morning I dressed and headed over to the embassy. I bypassed the door where there was a line of people waiting to see the Services Officer, even though that was the side of the building I was going to. Jack Roark had his own office that was down the hall from the Cultural Attaché office. I knocked on the door and heard, "Just a minute.", come from the inside of the office. The door had been locked, but soon opened with Jack Roark standing on the other side of the door to the small office.

"Come on in Whitley, have a seat." He said as he picked up some file folders out of the only other chair in the room, besides the one behind the desk. There was no connecting doors in the office and he apparently didn't have a secretary.

"What exactly do you do here, Mr. Roark?" I said as I took a seat in the chair, and he moved to behind his desk and sat down.

"Oh, this and that. Nothing very exciting really. How about you, do you like your job?"

"As a matter of fact, I like it very much, so much so, I just reenlisted so I could extend my tour here."

"Good. Good. Very good. That's what I like, a man who enjoys his job. How would you like to give your career a little boost?"

"Excuse me Sir, but I really don't know what this is all about. If you are going to offer me a job, I really do like it where I'm at."

"Well, I do have a job for you, but you won't have to leave the Courier Service. This job will only take a couple of weeks, three at the most. You see in the Diplomatic Service, we do a lot of unofficial favors for members of the service. Kind of like what you did for the Ambassador. You see, it's like being in a world wide club. Sometimes we do favors for other countries, sometimes for other agencies. It is a trade off, you never know when we might need a favor. Let's say, we needed to get a person out of a country, and we don't have a embassy there, but the Canadians or the Australians do. They do a favor for us, to repay one we've done for them, or will do in the future. You know, you scratch my back and I'll scratch yours."

"Yes Sir, I think I understand, but what does that have to do with me, I mean, I'm just a soldier in the Army?"

"Exactly, we're all soldiers of one kind or another. Some times we use diplomatic personnel or freelance professionals, and some times military personnel. What ever it takes to get the job done."

"I see, and Mr. Novak knows what this job is, and has OK'd it?"

"Well, Jim Novak doesn't know the specifics of the job, but he has OK'd lending you to another agency on a temporary basis, of course. If all goes well, this could really be a boost to your career and open a whole new avenue of advancement for you. That wouldn't be a bad thing, would it?"

"No Sir, I guess not, but what exactly is the job?"

"Even I don't have that information, it's *need to know* and I don't need to know. What I can tell you is you will be working for NATO Headquarters on an unofficial temporary basis, and I have been asked to make the arrangements. You probably know more about it than I do, they asked for you by name."

"By name? I don't know anyone at NATO Headquarters. I've only been there a hand full of times on courier runs."

"Well, of course, you could turn the job down,

but, as you know we are a member of NATO and if they want you bad enough, you could just be transferred there. I mean, like you said, you are just a soldier. Wouldn't it be better this way, you'll be back in a few weeks to a job you really like with a pocket full of kudos. All in all, I think this is a win, win situation for you. What do you think?"

"Since you put it that way, what choice do I have, but let me ask you a question. Just who the hell are you?"

"Me, oh I'm just a small cog in a big wheel. Nobody really, just another Assistant Cultural Attaché in the Diplomatic Corps."

I left the office and the next day I was on my way to Brussels. I don't know who Jack Roark really works for, but, I knew that was just so much bull shit about him just being an Assistant Cultural Attaché. I might be young and a little naïve, but I'm not stupid. On the train I was apprehensive about what this job was all about, and resented the fact that I was not allowed to tell anyone, not even Mr. Novak, where I was going. Scenarios kept running through my mind about who and why I was asked for by name, if that was even the truth. I just have Jack Roark's word for that, and I can't put my finger on it, but I don't buy the part about him trying to help my future out. They, who ever they are, might just need someone for a shit detail, and I'm the low man on the totem pole. I was so deep in my thoughts that I hadn't even realized that we stopped at the border, until the Belgian Customs officer had to ask me twice for my passport.

When the train arrived in Brussels I got off with my bag and was headed to the taxi stand in front of the station. As I hit the side walk out side, I was approached by a man in a well worn European suit and a heavy east European accent speaking English.

"You are Herr Whitley?"

"That's right." I replied in English and wondered if this is the guy I am going to be doing a *favor* for, and was curious as how he knew what I looked like.

"My name is Felix and I will be driving you." He said as he held out his hand to take my bag.

"That's alright I'll carry it."

"Very well, the auto is this way."

I followed him down the street a short way to an older model black Mercedes. He stopped and opened the trunk for my bag, then opened the rear door and held it for me, like a chauffer would, but he didn't look much like a chauffer to me. I got in then we drove off. Not much conversation until I noticed we were not headed in the direction NATO Headquarters.

"Where are we going, Felix? This isn't the way to NATO." I asked as I was starting to feel uncomfortable about the whole situation.

"Correct, I am taking you to meet Herr Schmitt first, that is my instruction."

"And who is Herr Schmitt, may I ask?"

"Günter Schmitt, he is the man who I work for and told me to pick you up at the train station and take you to meet him."

Well this conversation is going no where, so I just decided to sit back and see what happens next. We drove for about twenty minutes with no further conversation, then arrived at a small farm house on the outskirts of town. As Felix was opening the trunk to retrieve my bag, a man came out of the house.

"Mr. Whitley, I'm Günter, Günter Schmitt, I know you have a lot of questions and we will get to them, but now, please come into the house."

I went into the house and finally met some one from NATO, at least he said he was from NATO Headquarters. An Englishman named Ian MacNally and over coffee at the kitchen table, that had been served by an older woman, he began to tell me the most fantastic story I have ever heard. So fantastic in fact, that I figured it had to be true, I mean why would some one make up such a story and go to all the trouble to get me here to tell it to me.

CHAPTER 10.

Operation Norseman

I am suppose to take the place of a Dutch army officer and attend a meeting along with another Dutch officer. The meeting will be with a couple of Russians who don't know me, but most likely know what I look like. There will probably only be one face to face meeting, then my job will be done, because a few days after the meeting, the officer I am impersonating will have an accident and die.

"You mean you are going to kill this, Captain Van Norge?" I asked with apprehension.

"No, of course not. Van Norge had a premature accident and is already dead. You see, he can't die yet, it might spook the Russians and we need this meeting." The Englishman MacNally said, then continued. "Mr. Whitley, all you have to do is keep Gaylord Van Norge alive for another three weeks. That's all. It's really very simple, and there is hardly any risk."

"What do you mean when you say, *hardly any risk*. Look, I don't speak Dutch and why can't you get someone who does." I was starting to think these people are crazy, this plan is never going to work.

"You don't have to speak Dutch, the other officer will do most of the talking anyway. The Russians don't speak Dutch, and you two don't speak

Russian so the meeting will be held in either English or German. So all we have to do is teach you to speak with a Dutch accent. You won't be doing that much talking, and we have time to teach you how to sound like a Dutchman, enough to fool the Russians at least one time."

"I still don't understand why it has to be me?"

Günter Schmitt placed a large brown envelope on the table and said. "Open it."

I picked up the envelope and did as he said. I looked at the passport, driving license, NATO and Dutch Army identification cards. Then I understood why they wanted me. I was looking at myself only it wasn't me. Except for lighter colored hair, it was me, but it wasn't. It was like I was looking at my identical twin. I didn't know what to say.

"Herr Whitley, you must trust us, we know what we are doing. This will work, and it is of vital importance." Günter said with conviction.

"One meeting, and that's all. Then I can go back to Bonn."

"I assure you Mr. Whitley, we just need to keep Van Norge alive long enough to make this one meeting and we have almost three weeks to teach you every thing you need to know. Even Van Norge's girlfriend will go along. It cost us a lot of money but she is willing to help us pull this off. I understand your hesitation, but you can see for yourself why it must be you. You will never be in any danger and this operation is so very important." MacNally said as he went to the stove to get the coffee pot and refilled our cups.

"Felix." Günter said as he made a motion with his left hand.

Felix walked over to the table from the kitchen door, where he had been standing, and reached into the inside pocket of his worn out suit. At first I thought he was going to pull out a gun, but he came out with a flask and poured a little brandy into MacNally's cup then Günter's. He then tilted the flask toward me and I nodded, so he poured a little in mine as well.

"*Prost*." Günter said as he held up his cup.

"To a successful operation." MacNally said as he joined in the toast and we all took a sip from our cups.

Günter took out another envelope and slid it across the table to me. I picked it up and looked inside to find a large amount of Belgian money.

"Expense money." Günter said.

"There will also be the usual fee at the end of the operation. You know what you would call gratuity for services rendered." MacNally added.

Yeah, usual fee I thought to myself. There is nothing usual about this mess I have found myself in, but by accepting the expense money, I guess I have agreed to go along with this lunatic plan, not that I have any real choice about it.

"Good then. I will leave you in Günter's capable hands, and I'll be off. Mr. Whitley, I will most likely not see you again but be assured what you are doing is absolutely necessary." With that, the Englishman got up, put on his hat and left the farm house.

"Well then, *Herr Van Norge*, shall we begin." Günter said as he finished his coffee and motioned to the woman sitting on the other side of the room.

And begin we did. The woman, who I learned

was Frau Minsk, ran the safe house at the farm where we were. Frau Minsk was in fact a Russian Jew who had married a Belgian that was *in the business* before he passed away and she had taken his place out of necessity, I suppose, but anyway she ran the safe house now. She came over to the table and said. "Come please."

She took me over to the sink and told me to undress from the waist up. I did as I was told, not really understanding what was to come next. In a moment she produced of all things a box of woman's hair color, put a towel around my neck and proceeded to bleach my hair. I sat back down at the table to wait for the hair color to take effect and Günter started to fill me in on more of the details of the operation.

That is when I learned that Van Norge and Squadron Commander Heiden, who is going to be my partner in this madness, had been spying for the Russians and had been caught in the act. That didn't inspire a whole lot of confidence in me as far as Heiden was concerned. In fact the more of the details I learned, the less confidence I had in the whole operation.

While Frau Minsk was rinsing my hair, Felix had retrieved another bag from the Mercedes. I changed into one of Van Norge's uniforms right down to his skivvies, they didn't want me to be in possession of anything that didn't belong to Van Norge. When dressed, everyone took turns holding up the passport and comparing it to my new look. I have to agree, I don't think even Van Norge's mother could have told the difference as long as I kept my mouth shut.

In possession of Van Norge's papers and dressed in his clothes, I became Captain Gaylord Van Norge of the Royal Dutch Army assigned to NATO Headquarters. Felix drove me to my apartment and pointed out my car, it was a newer model light blue Audi in the parking lot in the rear of the apartment building. The apartment was neat and clean, sparsely furnished, typically European. I wouldn't have any problems from the neighbors because Van Norge didn't socialize with them since he is Dutch and they were all Belgian. The only visitors that ever came by were his girlfriend, Mare Van Meter who is also Dutch and works at a very exclusive woman's boutique in Brussels, and the cleaning lady who comes on Mondays. It would also be normal for Heiden to stop by once and a while, so his coming by would not raise any eyebrows from the neighbors.

I was off from my job at NATO Headquarters for another week so my lessons would start immediately since I had just under three weeks to get ready for the meeting. Mare would be by tonight and I would meet Heiden tomorrow night. I was given an emergency phone number to call incase something unexpected came up during the times I was alone, which turned out not to be very often. When the phone answered, I was to identify myself by saying Norseman Viking and ask to speak to Father Jon. Norseman is the operation and Viking is my code name and I have no idea who Father Jon is. Felix told me not to go out for meals, that they would be brought in for me. My days would be occupied by Professor Jules, he was to be my Dutch language and speech teacher, and my evenings with Mare, Heiden or another one of Günter's men named Karl.

"I have to leave now, oh, and if the telephone should ring, which it won't, but if it does just say "Hello" if the caller ask for Herr Vissell just hang up."

"Who is Herr Vissell?" I asked trying to remember all this information.

"No one, that will be the Russians wanting to make contact. Just hang up, that is the procedure. Then call Father Jon and let him know that a call came in for Herr Vissell. Normally you would call Heiden and he will make the contact, that is also the normal procedure, they call you then Heiden makes the contact. I must go now."

"Wait a minute, I haven't eaten all day."

"Well, you are Van Norge, do what he would do. Order a pizza, this is a big city, you know, they will bring it to you." Felix said as he walked over to the phone sitting on the bar that separates the living room from the small kitchen and pulls the pizza menu out from underneath the phone. "Order a number five, that is what he usually does, or did I should say."

"But I don't speak Belgian."

"Neither did Van Norge, order in English, they speak English, they are very international here. Tell them you are Captain Van Norge, at number 43, Bolbeck Apartments, and you want to order a number five, they know where to bring it, he orders from them all the time." He smiled as he headed for the door then said. "Don't worry so much, you will be OK. That is what you Americans say isn't it, OK?"

I scratched the idea of the pizza, and decided to look around the apartment. It was small but efficient, and perfect for a bachelor. The fridge was stocked with beer and I found some cheese and bread so I made myself a sandwich and opened a beer. I felt like an intruder snooping around someone else's home. I guess I really am, but in this case, I don't think the owner will mind. In the bedroom I found some personal letters, that I couldn't read, and sitting on the dresser I found his gold Omega watch. I needed a watch, since they had taken mine at the safe house. I tried it on, it fit perfectly, so I left it on. The closet was full of uniforms and a couple of nice suits, but I didn't care too much for his squared toed European style shoes. I kept snooping around, anything to keep my mind off everything that has transpired in the last few hours. I finally took off the uniform I was wearing and dressed in some of his casual clothes, got another beer, turned the radio on and sat down to relax.

The door bell woke me. I got up and looked out the peep hole in the door, it was a very attractive well dressed young woman. I figured it was Mare Van Meter from the picture on the night stand, so I opened the door.

The woman looked surprised and started speaking in what I figured was Dutch. *"Mijn God! Gaylord. Ik gedachte ji zijn dood.*(My God, Gaylord, I thought you were dead)"

"Mare? Come in please." I said as I held the door open.

"Mijn God. You startled me. I thought you were Gaylord, you look just like him." She said as she came in and sat her purse on the coffee table and the bag she was carrying on the bar. "I hope you like Chinese food, it's from your favorite, I mean, our favorite, I don't know what I mean. I just hope you like Chinese food."

"Yes, I do, thank you. I want to say I'm sorry about your boyfriend, and I know this must be uncomfortable for you."

"You mean Gaylord. I'm sorry too, he was a sweet boy. I will miss him, we had some fun together, but we were not lovers. Oh, we had sex many times, but we were not lovers." She said as she started removing the food from the bag.

"How long did you know him?" I asked as I was thinking that she didn't seem to be too tore up about the loss of her friend.

"Only three months, my friend, who is a secretary at military headquarters, thought we would like each other because we are both from Holland. He was a nice boy and we had some fun, but we were different people. He is, or was, a farm boy and I am a city girl. I like the city life, and I like expensive things. So you see, it could never be serious between us, just friends you know." She got a bottle of wine from under the bar, then continued. "Open please."

"Your English is excellent, where did you learn?" I asked as I picked up the wine and retrieved the opener I had spotted earlier.

"Almost everyone in Holland speaks English, and I travel to America at least twice a year. I go to New York and Los Angeles, I am a buyer for Madam Chardot's. I thought you knew that." She said as she got two glasses down from above the bar.

"Well, actually they told me very little about you, except your name and they certainly didn't tell me you are so beautiful. What did they tell you about me?" I asked while I poured the wine.

"Only that I am to keep you company, keep you

out of trouble at night, and teach you how to be a good little Dutch boy."

We talked more while we ate, and finished the bottle of wine. Mare impresses me as being a real free spirit and definitely high maintenance. After we finish eating, she said.

"What do I call you?"

"Gaylord, I suppose."

"*Ja, ja (yes, yes)*, of course, well Gaylord, I've got to get more comfortable, why don't you open another bottle of wine, turn some music on and I'll be right back." With that she disappeared into the bedroom.

I got another bottle of wine out and moved our glasses to the coffee table and turned the hi-fi to some slow easy going music. She reappeared in a couple of minutes wearing only a black slip, no stockings no bra, just a slip.

"So, do you still think I am beautiful, without my makeup, my expensive clothes and my hair down?"

"Absolutely." I said starting to feel the wine.

She turned out the light in kitchen, lit the candle on the coffee table then joined me on the sofa. A glass or so more of wine and she started getting frisky, real frisky. By the time the second bottle was empty, she whispered in my ear. "It is time for your first little Dutch boy lesson." She got up, took me by the hand and led me into the bedroom.

I woke up early the next morning and heard her in the shower, but I went back to sleep until I heard the door bell ringing. I got up, put my pants on and went to see who it was. It was Felix and another older man that Felix introduced as, Professor Jules.

Felix said that Karl and Heiden would come later, then left and school started for real. Jules was deadly serious about his job and I learned quickly that anything less than perfection was not acceptable. The main focus was conversational Dutch with more emphasis placed on how it sounded when I spoke, than getting my sentence structure correct. He said that would come later.

I spent four grueling hours with Jules before he left and said he would be back tomorrow. I was getting hungry so I looked through the bag Felix had placed in the small refrigerator when he came in. It was a carry-out order of noodles, cabbage and sausages. He had also brought two large bottles of beer, the kind with the flipper tops. It didn't look like Van Norge was much on cooking in the apartment, other than a few plates, a couple of glasses, two coffee cups and some silverware, there wasn't any of the normal pots and pans other than an electric skillet and a steam kettle for making tea or instant coffee. I placed the heavy paper plate with the food in the oven and opened one of the flipper beers.

A little after 2pm, Karl arrived and my Russian lessons started. Not so much as to teach me to speak Russian, but to recognize a few words and phrases. This was so I might pick up on what was going on if the Russians started speaking to each other. "You never know, it might save your life some day." He said and this was my first hint that they might be grooming me for more than just one meeting.

Karl left at about 5pm and Heiden arrived shortly there after. Heiden looked the military part except for his hair, which was longer than an American military man. It unsettled him when he first saw me, and frequently he would forget and laps into Dutch when we were talking. He had a whole briefcase full of photographs that we would go over repeatedly.   Mostly pictures of people at NATO Headquarters, who might talk to me and who probably wouldn't. For the most part, English would be spoken at the Headquarters, but I must speak with a Dutch accent, that was the trick.   Heiden was a nervous man, hardly what you would picture as being a spy. Maybe he was so on edge because he had been caught and was worried what would happen to his family, especially if the Russians found out that he was now a double agent working for NATO Headquarters.

My language lessons continued on a daily basis and Heiden would come over every other night three times a week. Mare would come over about three nights a week, especially on the weekends. Sometimes she would bring in food and sometimes we would go out to restaurants that she and Van Norge had frequented. A few times she would sleep over and we would sleep together. She seemed to have absolutely no inhibitions when it came to sex. A couple of times we went out clubbing, she loved dancing to the loud music and one of her friends that smoked marijuana shared it with her both of the times we went to Club Zeus. Van Norge had been twenty-five and Mare was pushing thirty and was my first experience with an older woman. She was definitely a wild child when it came to dancing, sometimes she would get up and dance by herself or with a group of her girl friends and it seemed like she knew everyone.

As time progressed, so did my language skills and my confidence. I thought, finally, I would be able to pull off the meeting, especially after my trips to NATO Headquarters as Captain Van Norge, went off with out a hitch. What bothered me now was the feeling I had, that they would not release me after the meeting was over.

CHAPTER 11.

Plan For Everything, Expect Anything and Ignore Nothing

The Russians agreed to Heiden's request to get out of the smuggling, they wanted to split up the operation anyway. Too many people were in frequent contact with each other. If any one of the players slipped up, it could bring down everything, even Valerian himself. A definite departure from normal covert intelligence gathering operations, even for the Russians. Heiden's request had made them see the error of their ways, but they still needed the drug smuggling to help pay for the spy operations that were ongoing. Besides it generates a lot of cold hard money that only Valerian is accountable for and his personal life style and finances have made a remarkable improvement since its inception.

Two days before the meeting in Paris was to take place, Heiden was contacted to make an unscheduled pick-up at one of the dead drops.

Office of Colonel Eric Goldman, Director of Intelligence for NATO. Ian MacNally and Günter Schmitt are in attendance.

"Why would they change the location of the meeting on such short notice, and why to Marseilles?" MacNally asked generally.

"That is not all bad. At least we know the location in Marseilles. It is a warehouse on the docks owned by a Bulgarian export company that is a front for the Russians." Günter threw out for consideration.

"How do we know that?" Goldman asked.

"They have used it in the past, only for meetings and never for drops that we know of." Günter said then thought for a moment and continued. "But they have never used it for anything to do with drugs or the Turks."

"That could be the answer to the question. They are starting over. Total separation. All new contacts, that is why the new handler, new codes, new drops, new everything." Goldman said with a new understanding.

"But why all of a sudden is Valerian not going to be at the meeting? Is he spooked about something or is it really as simple as the separation of the two operations and starting new with a new handler?" MacNally asked.

"It could be that simple, or it could be that Valerian has something else to do and just can't make the meeting." Günter said.

"I would be interested in what is so important that it would keep Valerian away." Goldman said.

"Me too." MacNally interjected, then continued. "Do we have anyone we can discreetly put on Valerian while the meeting goes down?"

"How do you feel about the meeting tomorrow?" I asked Heiden as we left NATO Headquarters to go our separate ways until tomorrow at 2pm, when we would catch the train to France together.

"I don't know, it always makes me uncomfortable when ever the Russians change anything, they are such creatures of habit, they hardly ever change their shirts."

I don't think he literally meant that they don't change their shirts. It must be a Dutch expression that the Professor didn't cover. It also made me wonder what else didn't get covered. Anyway, I told Heiden I would meet him at the train station tomorrow at 1400 hours.

I was thinking how much I love driving this Audi and how beautiful the city is as I headed to the apartment. I was also looking forward to tonight, Mare was coming over. We were told not to do anything out of the ordinary, especially the night before we left, just in case we were under surveillance. No surveillance had been detected, but just to be on the safe side.

Yes, I was nervous, and yes I was having last minute doubts, even though I knew I was prepared. As prepared as I could possibly be and the fact that the Russian we were meeting is a new one and had, presumably, never met Heiden or Van Norge in person. It couldn't be more of a snap and what could go wrong. That is what was bothering me, it all seemed too easy, but seeing Mare tonight would take my mind off of the whole deal, for a little while anyway.

The Marseilles docks, in a car parked down the street, in one of the parking areas between buildings two men watch the Jean Pacre Export Company warehouse. The two men are Borg and Felix waiting for their chance to enter and wire the warehouse for recording.

Felix has been here before and knows the layout of the building. If the meeting was to be held in the office on the second floor there is a problem, the office is heavily alarmed because of the large safe inside. The building itself was no problem, only a local bell alarm that can be temporally bypassed. The two warehousemen had already left and there should only be two more people inside, the fat Bulgarian named Balzak who runs the company, and the secretary who is also Balzak's mistress.

"OK, here comes the woman." Borg says as he watches the door with his binoculars. She turns left and crosses the street to one of the other parking areas.

A few minutes later Felix says. "I wonder what is keeping Balzak, he should be out of there by now."

They know Balzak is still inside because the woman did not lock the door. Just then the door opens and two men come out.

"What the hell, who is that?" Borg asks.

"Koscov. What is he doing here. This is suppose to be a new guy." Felix says as he watches Balzak lock the door.

The two men shake hands and Balzak turns left

and crosses the street, the same direction that the woman had taken, but the other man turns and starts walking in their direction.

"Are you sure that is Koscov?" Borg asks.

"Yes, yes. It's Koscov, he was at the meeting in the Salvagny Hotel in Frankfurt. Get down he is coming this way."

Koscov crosses the street and walks within 20 feet of the car Borg and Felix are hunched down in. He doesn't see them, he proceeds to a car at the other end of the parking lot then exits right in front of them. They duck again as seconds later another car comes to life from behind a truck and follows Koscov toward the entrance of the dock area.

"Come on, let's get started. You drop me off with the gear then go call Günter and let him know about Koscov, and tell him that someone may have Koscov under surveillance. Be back at the front door of the warehouse in exactly 30 minutes." Felix said as he was gathering the two cases that contained the recording gear.

Borg pulls the car up to the front door of the warehouse. It takes Felix less than 45 seconds to bypass the alarm and unlock the door, he then retrieves the two cases from the car and disappears inside. Borg pulls off to go call Günter.

Back in Brussels.

I parked the Audi and headed up to the apartment in anticipation of Mare's visit tonight. I showered and changed to some casual clothes. With the hi-fi turned down low and playing some *Beetles* songs, I got a beer out of the fridge and sat down on the sofa to relax.

Mare was running later than usual and when she did arrive I could tell something was wrong immediately. She was not in her usual light, happy, care free mood and when I tried to put my arms around her and kiss her, she pushed me away and said. "Stop it you fool, sit down this is serious. I have something important to tell you."

Stunned and in disbelief, I sat down on the sofa to hear what she had to say.

"Something is very wrong. Koscov is in Marseilles, he shouldn't be there, unless the Russians lied in the message Heiden picked up."

"But isn't Koscov my handler? Wasn't he in the Frankfurt meeting with Valerian?" I asked wondering why all of a sudden she had so much information on the operation.

"Idiot! You still don't get it. Koscov runs the drug smuggling operation. The message was from Valerian. You and Heiden are to have no more contact with Koscov, that is the purpose of this meeting. New codes, new drops, new handler. Do you get it now, Koscov should not be in Marseilles, he should not have anything to do with this meeting."

"Who are you and how do you know all this?"

"You know who I am. Don't be so stupid. Didn't I tell you I was introduced to Van Norge by someone at NATO Headquarters?"

I guess I am that stupid. I can't believe that it didn't occur to me that Mare was one of them and her meeting Van Norge was a setup for her to spy on him. God, I am so dumb. What am I doing here, just a country bumpkin that is way, way over his head. It will be shear luck if I come out of this thing alive. I believe anything people tell me, and I thought it was all going to be so easy, a snap I thought.

"Well, aren't you going to say anything?"

"What do you want me to say?" I said feeling like a real shit head.

"It may not be so bad, we have men there, they will protect you, and it all could just be some kind of miscommunication. Koscov could just be there to introduce the new handler. Or, Heiden may have dropped of a message of his own when he made the drop. He may be planning to double cross us and defect. Koscov may be plotting to get rid of Valerian. We just don't know and not knowing is what makes this a dangerous situation. But, like I said, we have men there, you will be alright if you remember your training and remain cool."

"Cool, yeah, that's me, cool. You people lie so much, I don't know who or what to believe anymore."

"Look, we've come too far. You have to go through with the meeting, we can't change anything now. Why do you think I am giving you this new information, we are not lying to you, we are all on the same side. If we wanted to lie to you, we could have just let you go to the meeting without telling you." She said in what I considered to be a sincere manner, for what ever that is worth, anyway I believed her.

To maintain normal activities in case we were under surveillance, we went out to dinner, then back to the apartment. We spent the evening going over and over details. I was given a local number in Marseilles for Father Jon, just in case. *Plan for everything, expect anything, ignore nothing.*, had been pounded into my head over and over for the past three weeks. I was glad to have the number, even if it was *just in case.* Now that I could no longer trust Heiden, it made me feel better knowing that there was a life line out there. There was however, no doubt in my mind, that if things did go wrong and they had to choose between me and the organization, that these people would drop me like a piece of expendable equipment and I would be left to fend for myself. I never felt more alone in my life.

Mare spent the night to make sure I didn't disappear at the last minute, I figured. It didn't make any difference, I couldn't sleep, and anyway, where would I go. I thought about how happy my life had been just three weeks ago, a job I loved, friends and a new adventure everyday, but this wasn't an adventure that I was looking forward to, or even could have imagined. Even seeing Master Sergeant Peacoe again wouldn't be so bad, if I can just get through this. I really had no choice but to go through with it.

Here I am, an American soldier, with nothing to prove who I am. My only identification belongs to a dead Dutch Army Officer, sent on a job by a person who is not in my chain of command, working for people that I am not assigned to. I mean how bad can it get, if you think about it, and I was thinking about it way too much, my mind was going around in circles and I finally fell asleep on the sofa.

The next morning at about 1030 hours, Mare woke me with a hot cup of instant coffee, then sat directly in front of me on the coffee table and sipped on hers. She is one beautiful woman and the slip she is wearing doesn't hide any of her charms.

"What are you looking at?" She asked.

"You of course, still captivated with your beauty."

"Ja, ja. We have no time for *vrijen vanochtend* (sex this morning). When you are ready I will drive you to the train station. But *bedankt* (thanks) a woman never gets tired of hearing, she is beautiful." She said as she leaned over and briefly kissed me then got up to go get ready.

I waited until Mare was out of the shower then went in to take mine. While I was shaving she was busy laying out the clothes she wanted me to wear. She will make someone a hell of a wife someday. I thought to myself, then it occurred to me, she could already be married for all I know.

"I think you will look good today." She said as she went into the other room.

I finished getting ready and dressed in the clothes she had laid out, then joined her in the living room.

"This is for you, *Fransgeld* (French money)." She said as she held out an envelope for me to take.

I took the French Francs out and placed them in Van Norge's oversized European style billfold that already contained the Belgian money they had given me, then looked at her questioningly.

"Just in case. Remember, *Plan for everything, expect anything and ignore nothing.*, and as far as Heiden is concerned, I'm am only Gaylord's wild expensive girlfriend that will do anything for money and was paid a lot of money to help cover up his death and to help with you."

"I'll remember." I said and remembered something else I wanted to do. I went into the bathroom and opened up Van Norge's passport and flipped to the stamped page where I had written Father Jon's phone number in Brussels. I turned one more page and wrote the number for Marseilles. I wrote both of the phone numbers backwards lightly and in pencil, not that it would really fool anyone. Writing the numbers down is something a real spy would never do, but then again, I am not a real spy and even though I had remembered the numbers, I didn't want to take any chances.

When I came out of the bathroom, Mare handed me Van Norge's briefcase, it was the European collapsible style, like a college professor would carry. All the men carry them to work, even the janitors. In Germany the Americans call them Schnitzel bags because the workmen carry their lunch in them.

"Don't forget this, you have to look like a regular business traveler."

"What's in it?"

"Nothing, only a business journal and a sailing magazine for you to read on the train." She smiled.

"That's right. Like Karl said, *look normal, act normal, blend in and no one will even notice you.*"

Mare drove me to the station in her Citron and I wondered if we were going to make it. This is the first time I have ridden with her and she scared the crap out of me. She might be beautiful but she can't drive for shit. We arrived at the station and kissed in the car, to keep up appearances, but I don't think anyone was watching us.

I was a little early but Heiden was already there, so we walked to the ticket window together and both bought first class round trip tickets to

Marseilles, France. We had about thirty minutes or so to wait and Heiden was nervous as usual and said he wanted to get something for his stomach, so we walked to the little shop and café in the station.

"Order me a small beer and I will be right back." Heiden said in Dutch then went into the small shop.

I ordered his beer and a coffee and sandwich for me and sat down at a table. Heiden came out of the little shop and popped a couple of pills and chased them with his beer.

"Are you OK?"

"Ja ja. I will be alright in a minute. I have to take my *nervositiet* (anxiety) pill." He said as he opened a bottle and took another pill and washed it down with the beer. I am sorry, this is a bad time, my daughter is having another test today. My wife called this morning and she is mad because I won't be there when she calls back with the results."

"What kind of test is she having done?"

"That's right, I forget, you don't know. She has cancer. She was doing so well until last month, so my wife took the girls back to Holland so Mina can see her doctor."

"I'm sorry to hear that, but you can try and call when we get to Marseilles."

"Ja, I will try when we get there."

"Well, they are boarding our train." I said and he stood up with me and we found a compartment in first class and settled in for the ride.

While thumbing through the magazine Mare had put in my bag, I started wondering how a guy like Heiden had got himself involved in this mess, but I thought better of asking. That last pill he had taken must be having its affects, because Heiden was starting to doze off. I was thinking about doing the same thing when the conductor opened the door to check tickets.

"Heiden." I said to wake him as I handed my ticket to the little man in uniform.

Heiden woke up long enough to get his ticket punched then went back to sleep. I yawned and did the same. A brief stop at the border to allow the French custom officers to board and check passports. On the way back the French officers will get off and the Belgians will get back on and do the same. We finally arrived in Paris and changed to the Marseilles train.

When we arrived at the station, we had time for Heiden to make his phone call and to get some coffee before getting a taxi and heading to the docks. The driver was real talkative and from what I understood of the conversation in French, Heiden told him we were in the export business and really enjoyed being in France. Thank heaven Heiden speaks French because I can count the words I know on my fingers and toes.

CHAPTER 12.

Look Normal, Act Normal and Blend In

Just before entering the warehouse area I noticed a string of bars and seedy hotels, the kind you find around any port city in the world. We arrived in front of the Jean Pacre Export Company just a few minutes before the scheduled time. I guess when we leave, we will have to walk back about two blocks to the taxi stand in front of the old hotel that sits on the corner just outside the warehouse area. There are a few vehicles around, but mostly the area looked empty. Heiden tried the door, it was unlocked, so we went in and down the dimly lit hall way.

Straight ahead of us were bathrooms the only other door was to the left. We went in, it looked like a normal warehouse with rows of large racks packed with boxes. To the right was a pile of wooden pallets, a time clock with a card rack and a hand full of time cards in it, next to that was an electric loader plugged into an electrical panel. On the left were a couple of large roll down doors and a metal staircase leading up to an office area that overlooked the work floor. Underneath the stair case were a couple of old tables and seven or eight chairs, an old refrigerator and a bulletin board against the wall. The main warehouse lights were not on, but the ceiling lights above us, below the office area, were on. We didn't see anyone around. I walked out toward the center of the floor and looked up to see if the office lights were on, they weren't, it was totally dark.

We both looked at each other as we heard a toilet flush and water gurgling through the old pipes. In walks a man carrying a briefcase similar to ours only a little larger.

"Good, good, you are here. Squadron Commander my old friend, how are you?"

"Comrade Koscov." Heiden said, and I could since that Heiden had not expected him.

"Please, call me Boris. We are friends, are we not? Gaylord, my friend. You look different, younger. You must tell me what your secret is."

I almost crapped my pants when Koscov said I looked different, but I kept my cool smiled and shook hands with him. We followed him over to the tables.

"Please, join me." Koscov said as he sat down, then continued. "We have much to talk about, so many changes, my friends. So many changes. Gaylord do you mind?" He asked as he pulled a bottle of vodka from his bag then pointed to the refrigerator.

I froze, I wasn't sure what he wanted, then I saw the tray with the glasses on top of the refrigerator. I got the tray and sat it down on the table. Koscov turned three of the glasses over then said.

"Swedish vodka, not as good as Russian of course, but I have gained a curtain taste for it." He poured a generous amount of vodka into each glass.

Boris Koscov was in his mid forties and had a definite east European look about him, but his English was almost perfect, only a very slight British accent. Not a bad looking man, he was dressed well and had a very congenial air about him. The kind of guy that could fit in with a group of working men or at a society cocktail party.

"Nostrovia." Koscov said as he held up his glass.

Heiden and I took a drink of ours, but Koscov finished his, sat his glass down and poured more vodka.

"So, Comrade Koscov, you are to continue to be our contact?" Heiden asked.

"No." He said as he took another drink and watched us to see what our reaction would be. Heiden drank the rest of his vodka, then Koscoff continued. "I will be replacing Comrade Valerian, he has been very ill for a long time now and is going back to the mother land to, retire, shall we say."

"I'm sorry to hear that." Heiden said.

"I thought you might be Squadron Commander, but don't worry too much. Comrade Valerian was a greedy fellow, and it is not healthy to be a greedy fellow."

I'm not sure what is going on between Heiden and Koscov, but it doesn't seem to involve me. I get the impression that Koscov is giving Heiden a subtle warning.

"Your new contact will be *Bulldog*, you may meet him in time, but for now, only through the new drops. Which brings us to these." Koscov said as he reached into his bag and pulled out two black license plate frames. "What do you think Gaylord?" He said as he slid one of them across the table to me.

"It looks like a normal mounting bracket and frame, this one even says Audi on it. Mine I presume?"

"Correct, but there is more, much more, Gaylord. Look at it again. And you Hans, look at yours."

I looked again, but other than it was a little thicker than normal, I didn't see anything unusual.

"Very clever our Russian inventers. Very clever indeed, watch this." Koscov took one of the brackets put it on the table then flexed up on the bottom right corner, and with a little pop, he slid out an envelope size compartment.

Mean while outside, down and across the street from the warehouse, two French policemen are questioning two men in a car, who appear to be loitering in a parking lot.

Two men come bursting in to the warehouse. One wearing a mask and carrying a machine pistol and the other not wearing a mask pointing a gun in our direction.

"I want the money and the drugs, right fucking now!" The one without the mask yelled at us.

"What money, what drugs?" Koscov yelled back at him as he stood up in protest.

"You first Russki." The man pointed his gun directly at Koscov's head.

"Alright, alright!" Koscov said as he held his hands up in front of his face, then picked up his satchel and tossed it toward the man with the gun.

The satchel landed on the floor and when the man looked down for a moment, Koscov pulled out a gun of his own and fired at him.   Koscov was immediately cut down by a blast from the masked man with the machine pistol and his gun went sliding across the table to the floor. Heiden was wounded in the exchange, but Koscov was dying if not dead by the time he hit the floor.

"Guns on the fuckin' table now!" The one in charge yelled.

"We are not armed!   We are not armed!" Heiden pleaded as he held his left hand over his right shoulder, trying to stop the flow of blood.

"If you are, you're fuckin' dead." He said as he bent over to pick up the Russian's satchel.

Then, two policemen come running into the warehouse with guns drawn, but they too are cut down by a long blast from the machine pistol. One slumps to the floor by the doorway, the other manages to get off a shot hitting the masked gunman in the head. The policeman and the masked gunman both drop to the floor with blood running from their bodies.

The gunman left standing, dumps the contents of Koscov's satchel on the floor, then throws it at Heiden and yells.   "Where's the fuckin' money, where's the fucking drugs?"

"There is no money or drugs." Heiden pleaded again, this time with tears running down his face as well as blood running down the front of his coat.

The gunman points his pistol at Heiden and pulls the trigger, hitting Heiden square in the chest. Heiden slumps and rolls out of his chair.   The gunman then turns to me and says. "I know you're not Van Norge, I killed him. Who the fuck are you? Are you a fuckin' copper?"

I opened my mouth to speak, but nothing came out, I didn't know what to say and I knew I was about to die. The gunman backhanded me across the side of my head with his pistol, knocking me out of the chair I was sitting in. Then pointing the gun at my head he demanded.

"Who the fuck are you? Are you a copper?"

I still couldn't get anything to come out of my mouth. Just when I thought he was going to pull the trigger, there was someone else in the room. I heard a man yell out.

"O'Finn, you murdering bloody bastard!"

The gunman swung around to see who was yelling. Then I heard two loud pops, and the gunman fell to the floor. It was then I saw the other man, he was dressed all in black with a watch cap pulled down over his face. The watch cap had a hole cut in it, exposing the man's eyes and the bridge of his nose. He walked toward me without speaking. When he got to the man he called O'Finn, he rolled him over with his foot and shot him again. This time point blank right between the eyes. The man in black looked at me for a moment then turned around and left, never saying another word.

I sat up. I couldn't believe I was still alive. I tried to replay everything that just happened in my mind. It seemed like it took an eternity, but everything must have happened in just two or three minutes. Then another gun shot went off hitting the chair I had been sitting in. It was the policeman that was slumped by the door way, he was still alive and shooting at me. Another shot rang out missing me. I acted out of complete and utter instinct. O'Finn's gun was on the floor right in front of me, I picked it up and shot twice hitting the policeman both times. He dropped his gun and rolled over, his head hitting the floor. I knew he was dead, and I knew I had to get out of here.

I got to my feet. I could barely keep my balance. I'll be alright when I get outside and get some air, I thought to myself. When I got to the front door, it was raining and through the rain I could see the police car down the street to my right with its blue light flashing. I went the other direction and crossed the street, going through an empty parking lot. When I got to the corner of a building, I had to stop and vomit. I was dizzy, but I had to keep going as I could hear the BEE BAH, BEE BAH of more police cars heading in the direction of the docks. I went around the corner and down the side of the building until I came to a loading dock with a ramp. I went up the ramp to get out of the rain, then I saw a stack of wooden pallets next to a dumpster. I felt like I was going to pass out, so I knew I had to stop. I looked in the dumpster and pulled out some cardboard and paper packing material, then squeezed by the pallets and behind the dumpster. I put some of the cardboard on the concrete and covered myself up with the rest. I passed out.

In the back seat of the police car parked down the street from the warehouse, Borg manages to pick open Felix's handcuffs. Now that they are both free of their shackles, they begin to kick at the door windows. Finally the window shatters and Felix scrambles to get out of the car just as two more police cars arrive. Felix starts to run, but he is quickly nabbed. Borg never makes it out of the back seat of the car. The two men are re-cuffed and placed under guard as the others start to search for the two missing policemen.

Two more police cars arrive on the seen. Finally someone checks the open door of the Jean Pacre Export Company and finds the carnage within.

Felix and Borg are taken to police headquarters for interrogation. They are questioned, threatened, and slapped around throughout the night, but the only thing they say over and over again, is that they were driving around, got lost, and pulled in to the parking lot to look at a map. The two policemen had handcuffed them and placed them into the back of the police car when they heard shots coming from the building down the street.

I came to, briefly, a couple of times during the night. Once to voices of men, speaking French, walking around the building shining flashlights, but I was dazed, confused, dizzy and exhausted. I knew I couldn't run, so if they found me there was nothing I could do about it.

It was midmorning and had stopped raining when I finally woke up to sounds of seagulls screeching, and water breaking on the rocks across the road from where I was. Noisy I thought at first, then I realized those were the only sounds I heard. Where are all the people, I wondered, then it dawned on me, today is Sunday and there would be very few people around. I knew I had to get up, so I eased to my feet pulling myself up using the back of the dumpster.

I carefully eased over to the office door on the loading dock. I looked in to see if anyone was inside.

I didn't see anyone, but I did see my own reflection. There was dried blood on the right side of my face and the tan overcoat I was wearing had several dried blood splatters on it. I took the gloves from my overcoat pocket and dipped them in some water that had pooled on the concrete. Using the door glass as a mirror, I washed the blood from the side of my face. There was a bruised knot with a small cut that had stopped bleeding on the side of my head, it wasn't too noticeable since my hair covered most of it.

I checked to make sure I still had my passport and wallet, then ditched the overcoat and gloves in the dumpster and returned the cardboard and paper packing material that I had used for a bed the night before. I walked down the ramp and peered around the side of the loading dock. To the left I didn't see anyone, but to the right, about two buildings down, I could see what looked like a couple of fishermen on the other side of the road. At the end of the building I looked across the parking lot toward the warehouse. I could see two cars parked at the entrance, a police car and the other an unmarked car, I supposed, but didn't see anyone standing outside. I took the opportunity to hurry across to the next building. So far, so good, I thought, but at the end of the next building I heard voices, two men talking and some clanking noises. When I heard a truck start, I looked around the corner in time to see a wrecker towing a car away.

The closer I got to the entrance of the dock area the more confident I was feeling. I just had to get by the fishermen ahead. It was an old man and a young boy fishing, when I got almost to them, the old man turned around and said.

"Bon jour Monsieur."

"Bon jour." I said, smiled, waived and kept right on walking. The old man turned back around and continued his fishing.

When I got past the last building, the road turned to the right and joined the main road coming in to the warehouse area. I considered which would be less conspicuous, a lone man walking out the main entrance, or turning left and going around the fence that doesn't quite go all the way to the water. I decided to follow the water front another two blocks before going up to the main street. I almost out smarted myself, when I got down a few hundred yards, my way was cut off by the back of a building that went all the way to the edge of the dock. The only exit I had now, was to climb a wooden fence and go through a backyard to the main street.

Despite having to climb a fence, a dog barking at me, and the garbage can I ran into, I made it out to the main street without anyone yelling at me. I turned left and continued walking down the street. This is definitely not a tourist area and I need to get out of here. At the next intersection I spotted a café on the opposite corner with a taxi stand and a public telephone sign in the window, so I crossed the street then crossed the larger one to the café. I ordered a coffee and asked about the telephone, about the extent of my French. The barman nodded toward the back wall where there was young woman using the phone. I paid for my coffee with a twenty Franc note and put the change in my pocket. I sipped on the coffee and waited for the phone to be free.

It was a good thing I had written the phone number down, because my mind was full of so many things that I couldn't remember it. I took the passport out and found the right page and repeated the number to myself several times. The girl finally finished with her call, so I walked over to the phone, put in 20 centimes and made the call.

"Father Jon please."

("This is Father Jon, who's calling.")

"Viking, Norseman."

("What can I do for you, Viking?")

"The operation went bad, everyone is dead, I need help."

("I will need time to check this out. Can you call back in one hour?)

"No, I can't call back, I need to get out of this area of town and I need help now."

("OK Viking, calm down, and listen carefully. Do not go to the airport or train station. Take a taxi to 634 Rue Saint Elise. After the taxi leaves, walk down the block, just on the other side of 628 there is a small dead end alley. Go down the alley, knock on the last door on the left. Ask for Father Jon, the challenge word is Music, the counter word is Violin. Do you understand?")

"Yes, I understand." I said and repeated the instructions back to him.

CHAPTER 13.

The Safe House

I followed my instructions, got out of the taxi at 634 Rue Saint Elise and waited for the driver to leave. I walked down to the alley and turned in. The alley wasn't very long, there was a flower shop on the right and a small antique store on the left. There was only one door at the end of the alley and it wasn't marked. I knocked and waited a few moments, there was no answer so I knocked again. Shortly I heard what sounded like someone coming down stairs, then the door opened.

"*Allo.*" Said the dark haired, olive skinned lady that answered the door.

"*Parle angalis?*"

"*Oui.*"

"I would like to see Father Jon."

"Are you here for music lessons?"

"Yes. I'm looking for a violin teacher."

"Come in, please. Up the stairs." She said then locked the door and followed me up the long staircase.

The apartment consisted of the back half of the top floor of the building that faced the street. It was old and dingy with the wall paper starting to peel. The lady said her name was Pilar, and she looked more Spanish than French. She told me I was to remain until someone came for me. Pilar said she would cook for me if I paid for the food. I opened my wallet and gave her a thousand Francs.

"Will that be enough?"

"For now." She said as she took the money, folded it and stuck it inside her blouse, then continued. "Come, I show you your room."

The back room looked like it was set up for music lessons with several wooden chairs and music stands. Behind an old painted podium was a large bookcase filled with sheet music and a table with a couple of violin cases. She put her hand behind the bookcase on the right hand side and pulled. The bookcase swung open, revealing a door that lead to another room. The room was small only about ten feet deep, but went the entire width of the building. There was a window and two beds at each end of the room. A large wardrobe stood in the middle opposite the door with a sink and toilet on one side and a table with four chairs on the other. Pretty grim I thought to myself, thinking I would be staying in here until someone came to get me.

Pilar pulled the bookcase closed and attached to the metal strap that span the back of it was another metal bar that pivoted. She swung the bar up and over into the supporting bracket on the brace, with the end of the bar lodging into a slot in the door frame.

"It only locks from inside. You must stay in here anytime someone comes to the door, and when my students are here. Don't worry, I only have classes twice a week, and you can shut the door." She said as she unlocked the bookcase and pushed it open. "You are sure no one followed you?"

"Yes. I am sure, I waited for the taxi to leave and there was nobody on the street."

"Good, come on then, I will cook for you."

I pushed the bookcase back against the wall and followed her back into the kitchen.

The kitchen was large enough and kind of an all in one room with the stove, sink and cabinets on one side and a sofa, chair, coffee table and a pair of reading lamps on the other. The kitchen table sat in the middle of the room and a small room off to the side I was to discover was the bathroom. The other room in the back of the apartment next to the music room was, I supposed, Pilar's bedroom.

Pilar was listing to the radio and kept stirring something she was cooking while she made coffee. When the coffee was ready she turned the stove down and brought the coffee pot to the table. She sat a couple of cups and a sugar bowl filled with cubes of sugar down and asked me something in French, then repeated herself in English.

"Do you want milk?"

"Yes, please. Pilar, how long do you think I will be staying here?"

She got a half full pint size bottle of milk out of the refrigerator then sat down at the table with me. "If that is you they are talking about on the radio, you could be here for a long time."

"What are they saying?"

"That two policemen and four other men were murdered at the docks last night and they are looking for a blond foreigner. It is not my job to ask, so I won't." She said while stirring the three lumps of sugar she had added to her coffee.

I sipped my coffee and wondered how they

knew to look for a blond foreigner. I thought about the old man with his grandson, the barman at the café, the taxi driver who brought me here, but none of them could be sure that I was the one the police were looking for. I regretted shooting the policeman, but I really didn't have any choice, I mean he was trying to kill me. I then tried to remember what the man dressed in black, had yelled in English, "O'Finn, you murdering bloody bastard.", could he be the blond foreigner they are looking for. My mind was going so fast, I couldn't keep up with it and I was starting to get the order of things mixed up. I must have been in a daze and was spilling my coffee until Pilar talking to me brought me out of it.

"Viking, are you alright, I think you are in fuzzy land."

"Yes, yes. I'm OK, I was just thinking." I said as I took a napkin from the table and wiped up the coffee I had spilled.

London, Office of Sir William Benchley, Director of Special Operations, for the British Home Ministry.

A message has arrived and Benchley reads the note.

DEAR SIR, I REGRET TO INFORM YOU THAT YOUR IRISH SETTER HAS PASSED AWAY. SIGNED/MARTIN

Benchley folds the note, then burns it in the ashtray on his desk. He then picks up his private line and dials a phone number.

"Carlyle, Benchley here, received a message

from Martin, mission completed."

Paris, Office of Inspector DeLeon.

DeLeon turns to his aide, Sergeant Butan, and says.

"We are going to Marseilles."

"Why Marseilles, I hate Marseilles, my ex-wife lives there." Butan says.

"Well, we are not going to pay a social call on your ex-wife. I think we have identified our mystery man, and he is dead. Probably killed by one of our Dutch drug dealers along with two policemen."

"Oh, Christ."

"And Butan, see if DCI Franklin from Scotland Yard wants to join us."

"Yes boss."

Belgium, NATO Headquarters, Office of Colonel Eric Goldman. Ian MacNally and Günter Schmitt are in attendance.

"For God's sake, Eric, I had a feeling this romp would get out of control. Just how bad is it?" MacNally asks obviously shaken.

"Look Ian, we both knew there was a risk, there is always a risk. Goldman replies.

"Yes, yes, there's always a risk. Just how bad is it?"

"I better let Günter fill you in."

"Well, I have more information coming in all the time, but this is what we have so far. The Russian, Koscov, and Heiden are dead, also two French policemen, and two more unidentified men. We don't know if they were working for Koscov or maybe the Bulgarian, Balzak, or they could be warehouse robbers. We just don't know who they are. Viking is in a freelance safe house. We put him there after he called in, saying every one was dead."

"Where are we getting our information? If you don't mind my asking." MacNally asked.

"From several sources." Günter continued. "Felix and Borg were arrested in the warehouse area, but were released by the Marseilles police this morning. Apparently they were in custody when the killings went down, so there was nothing to connect them. I also have an informant inside the Marseilles police that is keeping me up to date on the investigation."

"You say an informant, do we have any influence?" MacNally asked.

"No sir, I am afraid not, no influence, but I am getting information, that I am paying heavily for, I might add. It seems the price has gone up since two policemen were killed."

"Tell him the rest." Goldman added.

"You mean there is more?" MacNally asked as he pulled a handkerchief from his breast pocket and started mopping his brow.

"Yes. I'm afraid so. Go ahead Günter."

"The police are looking for Viking. It seems when word got out about the killings, a French taxi driver went to the police and told them, he had driven two foreigners to the Jean Pacre Export Company.

He identified Heiden as one of them, but the description he gave for the other, didn't match any of the bodies. Since Heiden had a Dutch passport, they are looking for a young blond man, possible Dutch."

"Any thing else?" MacNally asked, hoping there wasn't.

"Yes. We have to brief the Deputy Commander in two hours. We also have to figure out what to do with Van Norge's body we have on ice and figure out what our liabilities and options are. Not to mention, what do we do with Viking." Goldman said as he had visions of his career being flushed down the toilet.

"I have to go to Marseilles, and I need money." Günter interrupted then continued. "Money to pay my informant and I need to get money to the safe house, we can't risk moving Viking out of France for at least two more days."

"Very well, but make sure Felix and Borg disappear, we don't want the French police getting their hands back on them, and find out from Viking what the hell happened." Goldman said as he went to the safe in his office.

I spent a sleepless night in my hideaway with a bottle of white wine Pilar had given me when dinner was over. The events from *that* night kept rolling over and over in my mind and the harder I tried to keep things straight the more confused they got. After breakfast this morning I will have to go back to my room because Pilar has a music class. Pilar is a good cook, but not much on conversation. The situation left me with a lot of time to think, too much time. A thousand different scenarios about what would happen to me next kept invading my thoughts. All I wanted was for this nightmare to be over and get back my life as a soldier and back to my job and friends in Bonn.

Inspector DeLeon, Sergeant Butan and DCI Franklin arrive at Police Headquarters in Marseilles.

At the Marseilles morgue with the local police, DeLeon recognizes two of the bodies. Heiden a suspected drug dealer that has been under investigation, and their mystery man, who is carrying a British passport identifying him as Jack Hewitt. DCI Franklin knows the passport is a forgery, but as per his instructions, he doesn't tell DeLeon who the man really was.

Back at police headquarters, while going over some of the physical evidence, Butan keeps looking at the photographs of the two men that were arrested in the warehouse area then released.

"I've got it!" Butan says with excitement.

"You've got what?" DeLeon asks.

"This one. Look at it." Butan holds up the photo of Felix.

"Yes, he does look familiar, but where have we seen him before?" DeLeon studies the photo.

"The surveillance photographs from the airport, he is the man who was following Heiden."

Inspector Gerould, the local detective who is in charge of the investigation, immediately issues a pick-up order on the two men who were released. When Gerould returns, De Leon ask him to run down what he thinks happened at the warehouse.

"Both of the policemen were armed, of course, one of their guns was fired at the man with the machine pistol, killing him, but not before they were both hit by the machine pistol. The other policeman fired his gun twice, whether he hit the missing man or not, we don't know yet."

"Missing man?" DeLeon asked.

"I'll get to that in a minute." Gerould said, then continued. "The man with the machine pistol also killed the Russian, sometime before or after he shot the policemen. We found the Russian's gun, it had been fired twice without hitting anything except the wall on the other side of the warehouse. We found no gun on Hewitt or Heiden. Now, we did find a gun with a partial palm print and a thumb print that doesn't match any of the bodies. This gun was used to kill Heiden and shoot one of the policemen. A curious note here, although the policeman was shot with this gun he was killed by the machine pistol, but according to the Doctor, this gun was used to shoot the man shortly after his death. Haven't got that one figured out yet. The prints we found on the gun also match the prints from one of the leather cases found at the warehouse, and *there* is the missing man. Now, although he didn't take that gun with him, he did take the gun he killed Hewitt with, because it is no where to be found. That is what we have so far."

"How sure are you, that things happened just that way?" DeLeon asked.

"I'm not, of course, I'm just telling you what the evidence says so far. There are still a lot of unanswered questions. For example, what is the connection between the men outside in the police car, and what happened inside the warehouse. What are these license plate mounting brackets with the hidden compartments all about, and why would the missing man take one gun with him and not the other, I mean if you could only take one gun with you for some reason or another, wouldn't you take the one you shot the policeman with?"

"Maybe, maybe not." DeLeon said then asked. "How did the two men get released in the first place?"

"What could we hold them on, they were taken before a magistrate and charged with disorderly conduct and damage to the police car. They pled guilty, paid the fine and for the damage to the police car. We couldn't charge them with escape because there is no evidence they were ever under arrest or if they were, what for. The radio call from the policemen said they were assisting two men who were lost in the warehouse area, and that matched their story. The next radio call said they were investigating possible shots fired in the area. When the assisting cars arrived they arrested the men for kicking out the window of the police car. There was nothing to connect them to the mess that was found in the warehouse. They weren't armed and no fire arms were found in their car. The only thing that was found was a map of Marseilles and two cases of electrical tools and some electronic gear, both of which confirmed their story of being electronic repairmen and being lost and looking at the map."

"I see what you mean." DeLeon said then continued. There was no way of knowing at the time, that one of the men had a connection to Heiden, but you must get them back. They and the blond man who arrived with Heiden are the key to this whole thing."

My third night in the safe house, and I was sick of playing solitaire and watching French TV. Pilar hardly talks to me, other than to tell me when meals are ready. I don't think it is personal, it's probably just the situation she is in, having undesirables like me, staying for a few days and then never seeing them again. The next morning I settled in to the usual breakfast of croissants, jam and coffee, but today was different. Pilar had news for me, she told me that I was to have a visitor this afternoon. I knew she wouldn't tell me who it was to be, even if she actually knew. These people are professionals and are very closed mouth. I guess they have to be in their jobs.

Finally, shortly after lunch, came a knock at the door. I hurried back to my room and locked the bookcase behind me, just as I did anytime anyone knocked on the door downstairs. I heard footsteps then a knock on the bookcase. It was Günter, and man was I glad to see someone I know. We talked for a while and I told him my story. He then had me write everything down that I could remember. Günter said I would have to stay two more nights to let things cool down a little more at the borders. Before he left he collected all of Van Norge's documents I was carrying and told me that someone else would come to get me. He also told me that if it was someone that I didn't know, the challenge word would be Homburg and the recognition word is Reno.

CHAPTER 14.

And The Walls Came Tumbling Down

NATO Headquarters, Belgium, Office of Colonel Eric Goldman, Director of Intelligence. Felix and Borg are being debriefed. Ian MacNally is also in attendance.

After listening to their story, MacNally starts to ask questions.

"So you didn't see anyone entering the building after Heiden and Viking. Could someone have entered, and you just didn't see them?"

"They could have. It was starting to rain and the window was getting fogged up." Felix said, then Borg spoke up.

"Look, we were not there to watch the building. We were there to wire the place then retrieve the recording equipment after the meeting was over. We have done this many times, never any problems."

"Well you didn't do very well this time." Goldman said.

"We did our job." Felix replied starting to get defensive.

"You only did half of the job, you didn't bring back the tapes."

"How could we, the police were getting ready to leave when someone in the warehouse started shooting so they handcuffed us and put us in the back of the police car." Felix said, followed instantly by Borg.

"We almost got away, another minute and we would have been gone."

"Right, that is when the other police cars arrived. OK men, that's it. Wait for Günter, he'll have another job for you when he gets back." Goldman told them, but Borg wasn't ready to leave.

"What you said about half a job."

"Don't worry, you'll be paid the agreed upon amount." Goldman said.

"And the money we had to pay to get out of jail?

"Your expenses will be reimbursed. That will be all gentlemen." Ian MacNally dismissed them and they left the office.

The next day when Günter arrives back in Brussels he tells Goldman and MacNally what he has learned from his informant in Marseilles then shows them Viking's written account of what happened.

"These scenarios don't even come close to matching. Are the police incompetent or is Viking lying?" Goldman asked.

"I don't know and there is no way of telling with out the tapes." Günter replied.

"If you think about it, Viking's story does match the evidence, if you believe in the mysterious man dressed in black." MacNally added.

"Bunkum. It's ridiculous. Two robbers show up in the middle of the meeting, looking for money and drugs. I don't believe it, and if that is not enough, another man shows up and kills Hewitt then disappears. Total bunkum." Goldman says.

"Not so fast." Günter says then continues. "What if this Jack Hewitt is The Finn, and he wasn't part of the smuggling operation, but casing it, waiting for an opportunity for a robbery. He could have followed Koscov to the meeting. Viking says the man in black called Hewitt, O'Finn, before killing him. *The* Finn, O'Finn, could be the same man and we just thought he was part of the smuggling operation."

"OK, I admit it is possible, but who is the man in black?" Goldman reluctantly concedes.

"He could have been Koscov's man or working for Balzak, it really doesn't make any difference does it, and the police think there is a missing gun because they don't know about the man in black." MacNally says.

"If there really was a man in black. We need those damn tapes. What else do the police have?" Goldman asks Günter.

"They know that Koscov worked for the USSR Trade Mission, here in Brussels. The man with the machine pistol was a local hired thug, and they are running Hewitt's, Heiden's and Viking's prints through INTERPOL."

"They don't know that Heiden worked here at NATO Headquarters, do they?" Goldman asked.

"Not yet, but they are sure to find out. His passport says he is a Dutch military officer. It won't take them long to find out he worked here." Günter says.

"Christ!" Goldman says then continues. "This shit is going to land right on us."

"That is not the worst of it, what about Viking's prints? Remember, at the least he shot a

French policeman and may have killed Heiden." Günter adds to the pile of bad news.

"MacNally speaks up. "INTERPOL won't have his prints on file.

"That's correct sir, but in a murder case a Red Bulletin will go out, if they don't come up with anything. They will, as a matter of routine, submit the prints to all member nations, including to the American FBI, and as an American soldier, they have his fingerprints."

"We don't have a choice anymore. We have to bring the American intelligence people in on this. Only they will have enough influence to keep the FBI from identifying Viking. If the French get him they will never let him out of jail, and if he talks, we may be there with him." MacNally said and Goldman nodded in agreement then gives orders to Günter.

"Have the girl, get some street clothes and some workout clothes from Van Norge's apartment and give them to your men Borg and Felix. This is a three day weekend so have them get the body out of the cooler and sneak it into the gym here at headquarters, it will be closed for the holiday. Put him in the shower with the water running, it will look like he slipped and broke his neck. When the body is discovered Tuesday, I'll have it transferred to the military mortuary in Germany and that will keep the local police out of it. What else? Goldman asks?"

"What about Viking? We could eliminate him that would solve some of the problem." Günter says without batting an eye.

"Oh Christ no! Enough people are dead already. Give the girl his Diplomatic passport and the clothes he was wearing when he got here, then have her go get him. He'll trust her. We don't want him going rabbit on us. Have her take him to our safe house here in Brussels so we can control him until we get the truth out of him." MacNally says.

London, Scotland Yard Headquarters. DCI Franklin has returned to England and is in a meeting with Sir James Carlyle, Commissioner of New Scotland Yard.

"Sir James, I must tell you that I think we have been used, or more correctly, that I have been used to perpetrate an illegal assassination."

"If you are speaking about Sean O'Finn, I wouldn't if I were you. There are very sensitive issues here. Besides, the information I have says he was killed during the commission of a robbery."

"That may be, but the French are going to know we lied to them about his identify, when his prints come back from INTERPOL. This Inspector DeLeon is no fool. When Jack Hewitt is identified as O'Finn, an IRA terrorist wanted by us, he'll know we deliberately concealed that information and try to blame us for the deaths of the two French policeman."

"I see. Well then, you better beat INTERPOL to the punch. Call DeLeon and tell him that you brought a copy of Jack Hewitt's prints back with you and identified him as the terrorist O'Finn. That way he will just think we are inept, rather than being involved in some sorted plot. From what I know of the French and their arrogance, he'll buy it. Remember Franklin, always let your adversary think he is smarter than you." Carlyle says playing the wise old school master."

"Yes sir, I suppose that would be the best option. I'll get to it straight away."

"And Franklin, for your sake, this will end the O'Finn matter as far as you are concerned. Do you understand?"

"Very well sir." Franklin said as he got up to depart the office.

Well the day of my reprieve finally came or so I thought at the time. When there came a knock at the door downstairs, I got up and went back to my room. No heavy footsteps this time, but none the less, the tapping on the bookcase came. I was pleasantly surprised to see Mare.

"What are you doing here."

"Ja, it's me I've just come to get my little Dutch boy, of course. I have your clothes with me. Get dressed so we can get out of here. I'm sure you're ready to go."

"You bet, it won't take me a minute." I said as I didn't waste any time and started changing clothes while she was standing there.

"Bundle up the stuff you were wearing and Pilar will burn them. By the way, what did you do with the gun?" Mare asked while looking around.

"What gun? I don't have a gun with me."

"Oh. They told me you had a gun and I was suppose to get rid of it before we left."

"No gun. Just me."

Mare gave the clothes and an envelope to Pilar

on the way out. We got into the rental car and headed to the town where she rented it. She told me it was better if we didn't catch the train in Marseilles. Mare flirted with everyone, the ticket agent, the policeman on the platform, the conductor, and the customs officers at the border. I knew what she was doing. She was distracting everyone to take the heat off me, and believe me, Mare has the equipment to do it with. I have shirts with tails longer than the skirt she was wearing.

When we arrived in Brussels we were met by Günter and Mare said goodbye. I was, to say the least, disappointed. I don't know what I thought was going to happen, but I had visions of spending the night with Mare. Günter didn't have much to say as we drove to the farm house.

"How long am I going to have to stay here?" I asked as we arrived.

"Two days, maybe three, don't worry. Tomorrow two men will come to talk to you. A debriefing, you know what that is don't you?"

"I know what a debriefing is, but I have already told you everything I know, and I'm almost a week over due back in Bonn. You guys told me I would be out of here by now."

"Two maybe three days, don't worry."

Günter left me in the care of Frau Minsk and she took me to the upstairs bedroom, where I would be sleeping. The farm house was small, four rooms downstairs, including the kitchen, and the large bedroom upstairs. The room was large but cozy, even though there is no door at the top of the stairs. There is a large bed on one side of the room and a single bed on the other. There is a wardrobe instead of a closet, they don't seem to be much on closets in Europe. A couple of small tables with lamps on them and a couple of wooden chairs and that was about it.

A couple more days, I thought, that won't be so bad, especially after what I've been through. Just a couple more days and this whole nightmare will be behind me and I will be able to get back to my life.

Marseilles, Police Headquarters, Inspector Gerould's Office. Inspector DeLeon and Sergeant Butan are preparing to return to Paris.

"Inspector, I will keep you informed, and you Butan, I am sorry you didn't get a chance to visit your ex-wife. If you like, I can look her up and tell her how well you are doing, and how much more money you are making with your promotion to Sergeant." Gerould said and DeLeon put his hand over his face and coughed to hide his laugh.

"Oh please, Inspector Gerould, you are much, much too busy to bother with that. I beg of you." Butan said then they all laughed.

"Very well Sergeant since you put it that way." Well Inspector DeLeon, thank you for your assistance and say hello to Paris for me. Gerould said and they all shook hands then DeLeon and Butan departed. A few minutes later came a knock on the door and a policeman stuck his head in.

"Mon Chef, I hate to bother you, but Monsieur Balzak is here again. He wants to know when we will be finished at the warehouse."

"Tell him maybe tomorrow, after we do one

more search."

"Oui Chef (yes boss), I'll tell him."   The policeman says then closes the door.

About five minutes later Gerould goes into the squad room and tells the duty sergeant to arrange for ten men to be at the Jean Pacre Export Company in the morning for another search of the warehouse.

CHAPTER 15.

The Debriefing

The next morning I woke up to the smell of coffee and breakfast cooking. I got dressed and grabbed my shaving kit and headed down the stairs to the little bathroom just off the kitchen to clean up.

"Guten Morgen, Frau Minsk."

"Guten Morgen Herr Viking. Mochten Sie Essen?"

"Absolutely I want to eat, it smells good too. I just have to clean up first."

When I came out of the bathroom, a little old man was eating, so I joined him at the table.

"This is Willie, he takes care of the animals."

"Guten Morgen Willie." I said as I pulled myself up to the table. Willie just looked up and kind of waved with his fork. I guess he is used to seeing people come and go around here.

"Willie is not much of a talker, especially when he is eating." Frau Minsk said. She went on to tell me that he has a room in the barn but comes to the house for meals.

I heard a car pull up out front and shortly a knock at the door. It was Günter with two men he introduced as Herr Jones and Herr Johnson. Now there are two likely names for you. You think these people could be a little more creative considering the business they are in. So these are the guys that are going to do the debriefing, Americans both of them. If they weren't, they sure had me fooled. Johnson had no discernible accent that I could hear, but Jones, although he didn't have the look, had a definite Southern Californian Chicano accent. I thought to myself maybe he should call himself *Ho-nez* instead of Jones, and kind of chuckled to myself, but the humor was soon to go out of the situation.

Günter didn't stay, he just introduced the two men then left. Johnson and Jones sat down at the table to eat and Willie being finished eating got up to go back to his duties without saying anything to anybody. The two men didn't have much to say during breakfast, just general chit-chat and complementing Frau Minsk on how good the food was.

When everyone was finished eating, Frau Minsk started cleaning up. During which the time we talked, about nothing really, just general conversation until she was done. When she left to go tend her garden the tone of things changed.

"OK Viking, or do you prefer Whitley?" Johnson asked with an air of authority in his voice.

"Whitley. I prefer Whitley, that is my name."

"OK Whitley, let's get something straight right off the bat. We ask the questions and you answer. Understand?" Johnson asked and I nodded.

That's the way it started, they had me tell my story from the very beginning. Right from my conversation with Jack Roark to the time I arrived back here at the farm house. Jones would stop me every now and then and ask a question. Johnson was busy making notes, and when I was finished, he had me start all over again from the beginning.

"How many times did you make contact with Vilarian?" Jones asked.

"I didn't, I've never met or talked with Vilarian."

"Never?" Jones continued.

"No never, how many times do I have to tell you guys that."

"As many times as we ask, now what about Koscov?"

"What about Koscov?" I asked.

"Come on Whitley, the longer you resist, the longer it's going to take, and we've got all the time in the world, but you don't." Johnson chimed in.

"How am I not cooperating?"

"See. There he goes again." Jones said to Johnson then continued. "We've already told you, we ask the questions and you answer the questions."

This went on for four and a half hours, until Frau Minsk came in to start lunch, so we moved up stairs and started all over again. I finally caught on that they only asked questions that they already had, or should have known the answers to. About two in the afternoon Frau Minsk brought some sandwiches and coffee upstairs so we stopped and took about a twenty minute break. Then we started all over again. I just kept telling the same story over and over again, constantly being interrupted by questions designed to trip me up. If I wasn't telling the truth, I think I would have been in a bad way trying to keep my story straight.

Marseilles, *Inspector Gerould and his men are about to finish their fifth and final search of the Jean Pacre Export Company warehouse.*

The police had opened the two loading dock doors to let more light into the warehouse while they were searching and a few birds have flown in. They are busy trying to shoo the birds out so they can lock up when the Police Sergeant sees one of the birds pulling franticly on what looks like a long thin wire hanging down from one of the rafters near the front of the warehouse. He tells one of his men to get a ladder and climb up and see what the wire goes to, it is much to thin to be part of the electrical system.

"I don't know Chef, it is just a wire laying on top of the rafters."

"Well follow it, it has to go some where." Gerould tells the policeman. The policeman climbs on to the rafter and carefully starts to crawl along it.

After getting two more men in the rafters following loose wires, they have discovered three microphones all leading to a multi track recorder concealed on top of one of the overhead door mechanisms. Gerould climbs up to have a look for himself then calls down to one of the policeman standing around watching.

"Find Balzak and get him down here."

The inquisition continued into the evening only taking periodic breaks for the bathroom, coffee or to eat. After about ten hours the questions started to be more specific about the meeting itself. After telling and retelling what I could remember about the events, Johnson asked me why I killed Heiden.

"I didn't kill Heiden. Aren't you guys listening to me. The robber, without the mask, killed Heiden."

"OK, the robber killed Heiden, then you killed the robber." Johnson stated.

"That's not what I said. I didn't kill the robber."

"If you didn't kill the robber. Then who did?" Jones was mocking me.

"I told you a thousand times, another man dressed in black killed the robber."

"Yeah, yeah, yeah. A mysterious man, all dressed in black shows up just at the right time to save you and kill the robber. Everybody is dead and you didn't kill anyone." Johnson said then continued. "Well maybe you'll decide to tell us the real story tomorrow. Why don't you get some sleep and think about it and we'll start again in the morning."

So finally at midnight they went downstairs and let me get some sleep. I could hear them talking but I couldn't make out what they were saying, and I was too exhausted to care.

Marseilles, earlier that same day Inspector DeLeon and Sergeant Butan have returned from Paris to review the tapes found by Inspector Gerould and his men.

Gerould tells DeLeon that Balzak changed his story about not knowing any of the dead people and admitted that Koscov represented a group of investors who own the majority of the business, and that Koscov has requested the use of the warehouse many times for business meetings, but never any problems. He also denied knowing anything about the recording equipment.

"Why did he lie to start with?" DeLeon asks.

"He said he was afraid because the policemen had been killed, and he didn't want to be involved."

"He is involved. What makes you think he is not lying about recording the meeting? I wouldn't put it past the fat bastard." Butan puts his two cents worth in.

"From the look on his face when I showed him the equipment, I don't think he had ever seen it before."

"Bullshit." Butan said.

"Look Butan, since you are good with the ladies, why don't you get one of Inspector Gerould's men and go find the secretary, if she is with Balzak, take her somewhere and charm her. You know, tell her that Balzak is in big trouble, but you are on her side. Balzak knows a hell of a lot more than he is telling, so see if you can get it out of the lady." Butan doesn't like it much, he knows when he is being sent on a fools errand, but DeLeon is his boss so he obeys.

Gerould and DeLeon go through the recording. The Russian talking they know is Koscov, the man referred to as Squadron Commander is Heiden. Gerould stops the tape and tells DeLeon that he received a telex from Holland that states that Heiden was assigned to NATO Headquarters in Brussels. They then continue with the tape. The blond man that arrived with Heiden must be the Gaylord that Koscov is talking to. Then two more men come in, the French thug and Jack Hewitt. DeLeon stops the tape this time and tells Gerould that DCI Franklin called from London and identified Hewitt's prints as belonging to Sean O'Finn, a wanted IRA terrorist.

"That makes since, you'll hear his name later on the tape." Gerould says then turns the recorder back on.

This is where Koscov is shot by the thug. A single shot then a blast from the machine pistol. Then the policemen come in and are shot by the thug. Only one gets a shot off that must kill the thug because he is not heard from again on the tape.

"Now listen carefully, Heiden says that they are not armed, but a gun with Koscov's fingerprints was found underneath O'Finn. Then Heiden again saying there is no money or drugs then a shot. That must be when O'Finn or Gaylord shoots Heiden. Now O'Finn thinks that Van Norge is a policeman. Van Norge must be Gaylord. What do you think?" Gerould asks.

"Well it's obviously a drug deal that is being held-up by O'Finn and the other man. Maybe Van Norge and Gaylord are not the same man. O'Finn says on the tape he killed Van Norge and he thinks Gaylord is a policeman." DeLeon says then continues. "Gaylord could be a policeman, the place was wired and under surveillance, more than likely by the two men who were picked up and released."

"Yes, yes, but whose policeman, who were they working for?" Gerould asks.

"The Americans, it's got to be the Americans, they are always doing stuff like this without telling anyone. They think they own the whole world."

"Don't be too fast to blame the Americans,

listen to the rest of the tape." Gerould says then turns the recorder back on.

Someone else has entered the warehouse and yells at O'Finn, then two pops and someone hitting the floor, a few seconds later another pop. Gerould turns the recorder back off and says.

"That was an Englishman, not an American and those pops, I think was a gun with a silencer and the Englishman just killed O'Finn. Nothing else is said on the tapes but there are four more shots."

"Well if the Russian worked in Brussels and Heiden worked at NATO Headquarters in Brussels, how much do you want to bet that Gaylord is also from Brussels and possibly worked at NATO? You or me?" DeLeon asked.

"Why don't you go, your department has the funding, and I can't leave this mess yet."

"Good, we'll see if Butan comes up with anything, then he and I will be off to Belgium."

The next morning, we started all over again. Same questions, same answers, they were relentless. They kept accusing me of being involved in some kind of sub-plot trying to provoke me into getting mad and defending myself. I just kept answering the questions.

"OK tell me again about this man dressed in black." Johnson said.

"I've told you and told you, I don't know who he was. All I can remember is the head robber kept asking me if I was a cop and was about to kill me when I heard someone yell, and the man in black shot him."

"Exact words, are you sure he said cop, that is an American word but you said the man was British."

"OK, as best as I can remember, he said. *You are not Von Norge, I killed him. Who are you, are you a fucking copper?*"

"Now we are getting somewhere. That is the first time you told us that he said he killed Von Norge." Jones said then continued. "Now what exactly did this man in black say?"

"You mean you finally believe me?"

"Come on get on with it." Jones again.

"*O'Finn you murdering bastard.* That's all he said, then he shot him twice, but it wasn't as loud as the other shots, it was muffled, like what I guess a silencer would sound like. He then walked over and shot him again, in the head."

"That's the first time you said he called him O'Finn, but that's a problem, because my notes say the man's name was Jack Hewitt. Why would he call him O'Finn, are you sure it wasn't the other way around. Maybe Hewitt called the man in black O'Finn." Johnson asked.

"No. I'm sure the man in black called the robber O'Finn before he shot him."

"Tell us again. What did this man in black look like?"

"I told you, he was about six foot tall and dressed in black, including a black watch cap covering his face. It had eye holes cut in it. That's it, there's nothing else I can tell you."

I think they are finally starting to believe me when we break for lunch. During lunch Günter comes in and joins us.

"If you stay here much longer Frau Minsk will make you fat. What do you think?" Günter asked me.

"Well she is a good cook." Everyone nodded in agreement. Then Günter caught all of us off guard when he said.

"The debriefing is over. When you are finished eating, why don't you go upstairs and let me talk with Herr Johnson and Herr Jones alone."

I took my cue and thanked Frau Minsk for lunch, refilled my cup from the coffee pot on the table and headed upstairs. About five minutes later Günter came up and told me I would be leaving tomorrow afternoon. He also told me that the French police were looking for me for the murder of one of the policemen, but the man that was coming for me tomorrow would protect me and give me new orders. He apologized that everything had gone so badly, handed me an envelope, and said to follow my instructions tomorrow. He shook my hand and went back downstairs. A few moments later I looked out the window to see Johnson, Jones and Günter get into the black Mercedes and leave. I sat down on the bed and opened the envelope, it was two thousand dollars in hundreds and fifties. I thought to myself that two thousand is a lot of money, but what I went through was hardly worth it.

CHAPTER 16.

Hup Two Three Four

Brussels Police Headquarters. Inspector DeLeon and Sergeant Butan arrive with the sketch made with the help of the taxi driver that drove the two men to the warehouse.

No one at the police station recognizes the sketch, and a check of the names Van Norge and Gaylord didn't come up with anything until one of the clerks speaks up.

"How about Gaylord as a first name, as in Gaylord Van Norge?"

"Could be. What do you have?" DeLeon asks.

"Just an incident report filed Tuesday, but I don't think this is your man."

"Why?" DeLeon asks.

"Because this man is dead. According to the report a Dutch Army Captain Gaylord Van Norge, died as the result of an accident at NATO Military Headquarters."

"Who was the investigating officer?" Butan asks.

"No one from the police. A military officer at NATO Headquarters, that would be handled by their Provost Marshal. This is just a courtesy report." The Brussels Police Inspector says.

"Well thank you for your cooperation. Sergeant Butan and I will check in with the Provost Marshal then we will be off back to France."

The Inspector offers DeLeon and Butan a car and driver, and they all shake hands. Their visit to NATO Headquarters doesn't take long. The Provost Marshal identifies Gaylord Van Norge from the sketch and tells DeLeon that the body was found in the shower room of the gym Tuesday morning after the holiday weekend by one of the security officers. The Medical Officer that was called said he had been dead less than forty eight hours. The MO said the cause of death was an accident. Van Norge had apparently slipped while taking a shower. When DeLeon asks about the body, he is told that it was flown to Frankfurt, Germany to the Military Mortuary Headquarters for preparation and final disposition along with the MO's report. DeLeon informs the Provost Marshal that another of their men, Squadron Commander Heiden, is also dead. The Provost Marshal makes notes, but doesn't seem too surprised, he just asks the circumstances and wants to know when they can take control of the body. DeLeon figures it is pointless to question the Provost Marshal any further, because if the military was anyway involved in the warehouse deal, they are not going to admit it to him.

The next day I was growing impatient waiting for Günter's man so I went down to the barn to help Willie with the animals even though I wasn't dressed for it. I didn't do much really, mainly I just watched

Willie. About three in the afternoon a car pulls in the driveway and two men get out and one of them is an army officer. I watch them enter the farm house then I followed them.

"You Whitley?" Asked the guy in civilian clothes. He appeared to be in his late thirties, casually dressed, and definitely not in the military with that hair of his that came down over his ears.

"Yes sir, I'm Whitley." I said as I offered to shake hands. Neither one of them took me up on the offer. The civilian just looked at me and said.

"Take a seat, we've got some stuff to go over." I sat down and he continued. "My name is Roger, and this is Captain Walker he'll have some orders for you in a minute."

"Yes sir, do you mind if I get a cup of coffee?"

"Screw the coffee son. You are in a lot of trouble here. I don't know how you got in the mess you're in and I don't want to know. What I do know is that you shot a French policeman and we had to tell the FBI that you work for us to get your fingerprints blocked. Nothing is for free in this life son and you are in debt big time. So if the company ever has some shit job you can do, you will be called upon. Do you understand me so far, Viking?"

"Yes sir."

"Good, now understand this. Keep your mouth shut, none of this ever happened. I mean you tell no one. Remember all it would ever take is for someone to take the block off your fingerprints and an anonymous call to the French police. Now Captain Walker has some orders for you."

"You were never assigned to the Courier Service and don't contact anyone in Bonn, you were never in Belgium, and you were never in France. As far as anyone is concerned you have been and are assigned to the 3d Armored Division. You are to take a thirty day leave and when you get back you will report to the 3d Armored Division Headquarters in Frankfurt. Your personal stuff will be shipped there and will be waiting on you. And Specialist Whitley, if I were you, I'd stay the hell out of France. Here are your orders. Do you have any questions?" Captain Walker said as he handed me a large envelope.

"I don't think so. Sir, you know none of this is my fault."

"Look Specialist, I know you feel like your ass is out there swinging in the wind, but a lot of people called in a lot of favors on your behalf. So keep your mouth shut, follow orders and you'll be taken care of. There is a roundtrip ticket in there on a Lufthansa flight leaving Frankfurt tomorrow at 1600 hours, don't miss it."

"Yes sir."

"Well come on, get what ever you have and let's go, we'll drop you off at the train station. There is a bag in the car with some of your things in it.

I didn't sleep much on the flight back to the States. I was too busy thinking about not being able to say goodbye to my friends and losing a job that I absolutely loved. My life had been going so well, then all of a sudden like a bomb going off, my whole world was turned upside down. I wondered if the nightmare was truly over, or if I was on hold like an old can rusting away on a garage shelf put there by someone who thinks they might have a use for it someday. I hoped that the 3d Armored Division would be a new start for me and I would be able to put all this behind me and get on with my life.

I tried to enjoy my leave, but I still had a lot of things weighing on my mind. I felt like I was carrying that policeman in Marseilles around on my shoulders. I had to make a trip to Fort Knox while I was home. Who ever packed my bag put in a set of dress greens, but didn't include a shirt, shoes or belt and I needed to have Spec Five patches sewn on my uniform jacket. My time at home went by faster than I thought it would and soon it was time to head back to Germany. I was excited about going back to Germany and was looking forward to just being a regular soldier again.

I left home a couple of days early so I could visit the Statue of Liberty and the Empire State Building in New York City. About half way through the flight to Germany I finally fell asleep. When I woke up I realized that the weight on my shoulders was finally going away. I don't know exactly when it happened, but I knew I was thinking about that month in life less and less as time went on. Except for Mare of course, I think I will remember her the rest of my life.

At the Frankfurt airport I checked in with the Military Transportation Office and caught the bus to 5th Corps Headquarters at Gibbs Kaserne. At the transit station I waited for the truck that would take me and about four other 3d Armored Division soldiers to Division Headquarters at Drake and Edwards Kasernes out on the outskirts of Frankfurt on Hombergerlanstrasse, now there's a name for you, I think it means *The street where the people from Homburg live,* but I'm not sure. The truck stopped first at Drake, that's where I and all but one of the other guys got off. I guess the other guy went with the truck to Edwards which was located across the street. The other guys went their own way and I was directed to the duty officer at the AG (Adjutant General) building. I reported in and the duty officer pulled a copy of my orders and said I would be processed-in tomorrow and directed me down to the basement where the transit room was. The Sergeant on duty said to pick an empty bunk and lock my bag up and that the Mess Hall was still serving for another twenty minutes if I wanted to get something to eat. After dinner and back at the transit room a couple of the other new solders that had arrived earlier that day were going to walk over to the movie theatre so I joined them.

The next morning after reveille and breakfast I was sent upstairs to personnel to start my in-processing. When I arrived at the Personnel Office the Sergeant was waiting for me and told me to have a seat that the Major wanted to see me. A few minutes later I was called into the office and reported to Major Gammas the Assistant Adjutant General. He returned my salute and said.

"Have a seat Specialist Whitley. In my fourteen years in the army and most of it in personnel I have never seen a *Duty Soldier*. What is it exactly, that you do?" He asked as he was reading over my 201 file.

"I'm sorry sir, I'm not at liberty to say."

"It says here that you have been here for a year and a half, US Army Europe - unassigned is all it says. Where have you been for eighteen months? Yeah, yeah, I know. You are not at liberty to say. Now where have I heard that before. Is there anything you can say?"

"No sir, except that I'm here and ready to be assigned."

"Well I have received a classified message on you, it says that you are to be assigned to Division Headquarters for the remainder of your three year tour. Did you know about that?"

"No sir, I didn't"

"Well let me ask you this question, is he a Congressman, a Senator or a General?"

"I'm sorry sir, I don't understand."

"Your relative that is pulling all these strings. Is he a Congressman, a Senator or a General?"

"No sir, none of the above. I'm just a plain soldier. I don't have any important relatives."

"Alright Whitley, no more games. I don't know if you are CID or a rat for the Inspector General, it doesn't make any difference to me. The message says you are to be assigned to Division Headquarters so that's what I'm going to do. I don't have any slots for *Duty Soldiers*, so I will assign you, on paper anyway, in your secondary MOS, 97C. There are two vacant slots in the G2's office (Asst. Chief of Staff for Intelligence) but since the G4 (Asst. Chief of Staff for Logistics) is short of administrative personnel, you will be working there. You can type, your file says you took a typing course at Fort Sill, is that correct?"

"Yes sir, that's correct."

"OK Whitley, that will be all, see Sergeant Straminsky outside and finish your processing."

I spent the rest of the morning going from place to place processing-in and had noticed that everyone was wearing scarves or ascots tucked into their fatigue shirts. They were in different colors, the MP's wore green, the Medic wore maroon, but most everyone else was wearing yellow ones. When I got to Sergeant Fong at Finance, he spent a lot of time going over my records, and filling out forms for me to sign.

"You have a lot of money coming to you Whitley, twenty six days of per diem and three unpaid travel vouchers. Do you want this in cash or a check?"

"A check will be fine Sergeant Fong. I have to find the nearest American Express office anyway, I need to have my checking account moved."

"Well you are in luck, there's a branch bank across the street at Edwards Kaserne. You are finished here Specialist Whitley. Take this voucher to the cashiers cage down the hall and they will issue you a check."

Finished with my processing I went back to Sergeant Straminsky's office and picked up my assignment orders. He directed me to the baggage room to pick up the rest of my things that had been shipped from Bonn, then to the Headquarters Company the building next to the main gate and told me to go check-in. There I filled out a mail locator card, was assigned a weapon at the arms room, received my gasmask and field gear and picked up bed linen at the supply room. I received a room assignment on the third floor and had to make two trips to get all my stuff up there. It was a four man room, but I was to find out later that two of the guys were short-timers and would be leaving in about a month. According to name tags on the door everyone in the room also worked at G4 and as I changed into

fatigues which is the duty uniform I noticed a couple
of the yellow scarves laying on the small table in the
room. I figured I'd better borrow one, I didn't want
to be out of uniform when I reported in to my new job
for the first time. I had never seen these things
before, we didn't wear them in the states. It was
more of a dickey than a scarf, just a piece of material
with a collar that snapped in the back and I must
admit they did look sharp.

The Division Headquarters building was also
next to the main gate, just on the other side of the
driveway from Headquarters Company. The sign
inside the front door said that G2, G3 and G4 were
located on the second floor so I went up the steps to
find the G4. I met Sergeant Major Berkie and he took
me in to meet the big boss, at least as far as I'm
concerned. The ACofS G4, was Lt. Colonel "Ace"
Bowen and he welcomed me to the staff and told the
Sergeant Major to get me squared away and I could
start work tomorrow. The Sergeant Major took me
around to some of the other offices that were part of
G4 and introduced me to some of the staff. He then
asked me if I had any money, which kind of caught
me off guard, and when I replied yes, he told me to
go get a hair cut and go to the PX and buy a
camouflage scarf, he said people on the General Staff
wear camo not yellow. That was my first meeting
with Sergeant Major Berkie, I got the feeling that if I
had told him I didn't have any money he would have
pulled some out of his own pocket and given it to me.
I was to grow to have a lot of respect in the months to
come for both the Sergeant Major and Lt. Col.
Bowen.

CHAPTER 17.

3d Armored Division, Spearhead,
The Elvis Presley Division

Oh yeah, I'm back in the Army now. Drake Kaserne has a movie theater, a gym, library and enlisted/NCO Clubs. At Edwards where the married housing is, there's a PX, a snack bar, a USO Service Club and an American Express Bank. Closer to town there is a big PX and commissary, another movie theater, and the big NCO Club called the Topper. Yep, there is everything a young soldier needs, too bad we don't get to use them. It is dark when we go to work in the morning and dark when we get off at night. Missing dinner is almost a daily occurrence because the Mess Hall is usually finished serving by the time we get off work. If you need to get a haircut, drop-off or pick-up laundry or dry cleaning you have to do it in the daytime instead of going to lunch. We do get Sundays off but the PX, library and Ed Center are closed on Sundays. Most everyone gets off early on Saturdays, but we never seem to get out of the office until at least 1600 hours. Now if you are married you get over like a snot rag, because it doesn't make any difference what time the Mess Hall closes if you go home to eat. Married guys don't stand reveille at 0600 and only guys living in the barracks pull duty on the weekends. The difference between buck Sergeants and Spec Fives, even though they are the same pay grade, is ridiculous. Buck Sergeants pull Sergeant of the Guard, while Spec Fives stand guard. That means Spec Fives pull guard duty eight times more often than buck Sergeants. While buck Sergeants and Spec Fives both pull CQ (Charge of Quarters) duty, buck Sergeants don't pull Staff Duty NCO, but Spec Fives pull Staff Duty Runner. There is a definite advantage to having three stripes on your arm instead an eagle with a stripe over the top of it. The only time they are equal is when it comes to paying NCO Club dues or supervising a shit detail.

Believe it or not I do like it here, you get used to working so many hours, you just don't have much of a social life. Now there are those occasional Saturday nights when I'm not on the duty roster for something, I do go out and howl like a wild dog, and it is probably fortunate that it only happens about once a month. Then there are the monthly alerts, you never know when that siren is going to go off in the middle of the night and you have to jump out of bed, put on your field gear, draw your weapon and go get the trucks out of the motor pool then go load out the office. The married guys really hate alerts, because they have to get out of their warm beds, listen to their wives bitch, hunt for their shit and lug it over to Division Headquarters, because they are not allowed to drive their cars over during alerts. The G4 section has four vehicles. The Colonel's jeep, which Spec Four Ray Lawson, one of my room mates, drives, then there's the Colonel's expandable van that I drive, a 2 ½ ton truck and a ¾ ton truck. Ray would get the jeep and go get in the convoy line, the other trucks we would take to our place in front of Headquarters and start loading out the office. Now no mater how fast we did this, the Sergeant Major would always be at Headquarters before us. I always thought he got the heads-up when the alerts were going to be, but he would never own up to it. Sergeant Major Berkie is no spring chicken but he is always in there humping and helping us peons load the trucks. Once loaded, we would go get in the convoy line and wait for the order to move out. Most of the time the alert would be cancelled and we would go unload everything. Some times we would actually drive in convoy out to one of the training areas just to have the alert cancelled when we got there. At least once a year an alert would start field training exercises and we would go set up in the field, live in tents and do our regular jobs, for one week to one month. A lot of the guys would bitch and complain, but I enjoyed being in the field, because the Officers and Senior NCOs don't have their wives to cook for them and there is no way they are going to miss a meal, like they make us peons do back at Drake. So when 1700 hours comes, the work day is over.

Elvis Presley was gone by the time I got to the 3d Armored Division, but a lot of the old Sergeants were around when he was here, and every single one of them has at least one Elvis story to tell. I loved listening to the stories, especially in the field, in our tent huddled up around the stove trying to stay warm at night. Yes I know that a lot of the stories are more bullshit than truth, but I still love listening to them.

Cassius "The Draft Dodger" Clay came to Frankfurt while I was here to fight Mildenburger, and he made a big stink because they wouldn't let him and his entourage into the Topper NCO Club. I'm glad they wouldn't let him in. As far as I'm concerned, he didn't have the right to come in to an American Military NCO Club. He wasn't here on a USO tour, as if they would even have the draft dodger. He was here for his own personal gain and was booed when he tried to go to some of the Germans clubs, so why should we have him. In fact most of us were hoping that Mildenburger would knock the crap out of him, but it didn't go down that way.

Lt. Col. Bowen's wife passed away after a long illness and we could all tell he was kind of lost without her, but after a few weeks you couldn't blow his ass out of the office with a stick of dynamite, and of course no one could leave the office before him, so if the days were long before, we are putting in monstrous hours now. For the troops living in the barracks, our day starts at 0500 hours in the morning and we were not getting out of the office until midnight some times. Even the Officers were starting to show the wear and were complaining. I was tickled the day Sergeant Major Berkie told me that I would be leaving the main office to work with the Supply and Maintenance Detachment. They had their own offices over at Edwards Kaserne co-located with the Division Support Command and over there when quitting time comes, they go home.

I spent my days doing fleet mileage and *Forever Amber* reports. All the tanks in the Division are the new M60A1 tanks, except one Battalion that still has the old M48 tanks and no matter what you do to them, they will never have a *green* readiness status because of age or engine hours or lack of non-essential spare parts. There inclusion in Division readiness reports was bringing the Division's overall combat readiness score down and the Commanding General was raising hell, he didn't want to know why the score was down, he just wanted it fixed. So since the M48 tanks are combat operational, even though they are technically classified *amber*. I came up with the idea to take the combat operational *amber* tanks out of the Division's combat readiness report and list them separately on a combat ready but *Forever Amber* report. All smoke and mirrors of course, but the Division's combat readiness score improved almost seventeen points. Once Fifth Corps Headquarters approved the new way of reporting the Commanding General was happy and that made the entire General Staff happy. I receive my first Army Commendation Medal for my efforts.

Spearhead to pea head is a curious tradition practiced by Privates and Spec Fours when they become two digit midgets. All the troops have count down calendars telling how many days they have until they leave. When they reach 99 days left they become two digit midgets and the tradition is that they take a razor blade and tweezers and pull the threads out from the *S* and the *R* on their shoulder patches. So now their 3d Armored Division patches read *pea head* instead of *Spearhead*. All the NCOs and Officers must know this is going on, but no one says a word. The practice is just accepted as one of those unspoken traditions.

One day while I was still at the G4 main office I received some forwarded mail from Bonn. Of course the original address had been blacked out so you couldn't read it, but some of the letters were from Aimee Baker, Judge Fairchild's nanny. I had shamefully ignored her previous letters, but this time I wrote her back and have been carrying on a correspondence with her for the past several months with a promise to come and see her when I get back to the States. My days with the 3d Armored Division are growing few and I will be leaving next month, but I don't have my new assignment orders yet. When I was down to about ten days left, I got a call to report to personnel to pick up my orders and start out-processing. I was expecting to be stationed Stateside since I was coming from a three year overseas tour, but to my amazement I was being assigned to Vietnam as a 97C Intelligence Annalist my secondary MOS. I had assumed that I would be reassigned in my new primary MOS of 71L Administrative Specialist. When I questioned the Personnel Officer about the situation he told me that there was a critical shortage in Vietnam and all available 97Cs are being reassigned, school trained or not. So good-bye Germany and Vietnam here I come.

I was sorry to leave Germany, I really loved it there and I will miss the Gasthaus down the street from the Kaserne and the carry-out pizza place run by the Turkish family, the best pizza I think I have ever had, but life goes on and it's time to move on to a new adventure. I just hope I get to come back to Germany someday.

While at home on leave, I received a letter from the Department of the Army. The letter contained orders promoting me to Staff Sergeant but it didn't change my assignment orders. I was surprised because I was not due for promotion and remembered that Captain Walker said I would be taken care of if I kept my mouth shut about Marseilles. I wondered if *they* were still keeping track of me or if the promotion was due to 97C being a critical MOS. I guess I will only find *that* out if and when Viking is ever contacted.

CHAPTER 18.

On My Way

I spend a couple of weeks at home which included a trip out to Fort Knox to update my uniforms with my new Staff Sergeant stripes, then headed west. I wanted time to see Aimee, it was more at her persistence than anything else, I mean I like her well enough, but I'm certainly not in love with her. I also want to visit with my Uncle O'Dell and family who live in Los Angeles, before going to Vietnam. I caught a flight out of Louisville with a three hour layover in Phoenix then on to Los Angeles. While in Phoenix I called the Fairchild residence in San Diego.

(*"Hello, Fairchild's."*)

"Hello, may I speak to Aimee Baker please?"

(*"I'm sorry, Aimee is not at home right now, may I ask who's calling?"*)

"Yes this is Ron Whitley. Can you tell her that I called and will try and call back?"

(*"Ron, this is Linda. Where are you?"*)

"Hi, Mrs. Fairchild, I'm in Phoenix right now, but I have a flight in about two hours."

(*"Linda please, call me Linda. Are you coming this way? Can we pick you up at the airport?"*)

"Well yes and no. I'm actually flying in to LAX."

("Can't you change your flight to San Diego? That way all you have to do is call and we will come and get you.")

"Well Ma'am, actually I have a rental car reserved and will drive down if that's OK. I'll be coming back to LA to visit family before I leave."

("Stop that Ma'am stuff, you make me feel like an old lady, call me Linda, I insist. Do you know how to get here?")

"No, but I'm good at directions."

("We are only fifteen minutes from downtown, so stop anywhere and call and I'll come and meet you and you can follow me to the house.")

"It might be late when I get there."

("Don't worry about it. Just call.")

After picking up the car at LAX I headed down to San Diego. The traffic is terrible, even at this time in the evening, it seemed like it was going to take more time just getting out of the airport than the actual drive, but it was a pleasant evening and a clear sky after I got out of the city. I rolled down the window and just relaxed while driving and enjoyed the occasional salt air breeze that would come and go. The radio station I had been listening to drifted out and was replaced by a station playing Mexican music and it fit the good, if not festive, mood I found myself in. I was looking forward to seeing Aimee again, but a little apprehensive because her interest in me seemed to be much more than my interest in her. I do like Aimee and she is such a sweet girl that the last thing in the world I want to do is lead her on. Leaving for Vietnam in a couple of weeks should give me the means I need to see her again and fulfill the promise I made, while avoiding any entanglements.

I had arrived in San Diego almost before I realized and had to take the second exit. I headed to the downtown area and found an all night gas station and bodega with a hand full of Sailors handing around so I figured it would be a good place to call from. I sat in the car and sipped on the coffee I had purchased from the bodega. About twenty minutes had passed when a car pulled in and what appeared to be a young girl dressed in shorts and her blond hair pulled back in a ponytail got out and walked over to my car. It was Linda Fairchild, and I damn near didn't recognize her. It was hard to believe this was the same sophisticated and immaculately dressed lady I had met at the Embassy in Bonn, but that Jasmine perfume of hers gave the truth away. She is just as beautiful, but a lot younger than I remember. To think of this goddess being the mother of five kids, even if the five include two sets of twins, is just unbelievable.

I don't know why, but I had envisioned the house being somewhere beside the ocean, but I was wrong. I followed her Mustang convertible through the gates of one of those exclusive estates. A left then a right, then we pulled into the driveway of a very large Colonial style home with a large four car attached garage on one side and what looked like a very large sun room on the other. As we approached the garage both of the double doors came up, she pulled in to park and motioned for me to do the same. As I pulled in the doors came down, then the inside door to the house opened and I could see a middle age Mexican woman holding the door open.

"Ron this is Carla. Carla this is the Mister

Whitley, Aimee's friend, he will be staying with us for a while. Why don't you take him into the kitchen and fix him something to eat while I go up and check on the kids."

"OK señora Linda. Señor Ron, I hear so much about you."

I followed Carla and Linda through the combination mud and laundry room into the kitchen, then Linda continued on down the hall and up a small staircase at the end. Carla was busy heading up what was probably leftovers from dinner, talking all the time. When I asked her about Aimee, she said that she wouldn't be back until tomorrow. Soon Linda reappeared as Carla was placing a plate of food in front of me.

"You want anything else señor Ron?"

"Oh no, thank you Carla, this is excellent."

Carla smiled and said goodnight and headed down the hall. "Goodnight Carla, thank you for watching the kids for me." Linda called after her.

Linda and I talked for a while. When I finished eating she fixed a pitcher of Margaritas, that's when she told me that if I had come four days earlier I would have been able to see Casey and Lacy. Aimee had taken the girls back to the school in Switzerland and should be arriving back tomorrow sometime. She is going to call when she gets to New York. The Judge left for his semi-annual fishing trip right after the girls left, and is in a boat with his fishing buddies somewhere off the coast of Mexico fishing for Bonito. By the time the first pitcher was gone, she had told me almost her whole life story. Like how she met the Judge, that's what she called him, when she was eighteen and had just been named Miss

Orange County and was going to compete in the Miss California Contest. He was already a judge even then, only a State Judge in Anaheim, and how she fell madly in love with him. She forego the Miss California competition for the society wedding of the year. Less than a year later came Casey and Lacy, three years went by then Mary came along. Then the Federal Judgeship and the move to San Diego. Four years later came another set of twins, and that is when she put her foot down, no more kids.

By the time the second pitcher was almost gone we were up to Carla, who is a widow, being with them since they moved to San Diego and Conchita, Carla's daughter who goes by Connie and is away attending law school at UCLA. Aimee came from England to help out with Dino, which is short for Darious, and Dannie when they were just born and has become a member of the family too. Just one big happy home full of girls, with the exception of Dino who is completely spoiled by all the women around.

"The Judge, here's to the Judge, bless his sweet old behind." Linda said as she finished off the last of the second pitcher, then continued. "He pays for all this, but is never around to enjoy it. Between fishing every time he has a clear spot on his calendar, golf every weekend and not coming home after work until ten or eleven at night when he is on the bench. I tell you, if it wasn't for Carla and Aimee I would go crazy around here." She reached across the table and squeezed my hand and said. "Well, it's getting late and I'm sure you're tired of listing to me bitch, I better get you situated."

I got up to go get my bag out of the car and the Margaritas finally hit me. I steadied myself, retrieved my bag and followed her through a formal dining room and living room.

"I could put you in Connie's room off the kitchen or Casey and Lacy's room upstairs, but it gets awful noisy around here in the mornings so I'm going to put you at the other end of the house in the small bedroom off the den." She said as we walked by the large staircase in the front of the house, then down another hall. The hallway opened into what must be the large sun room I saw when we pulled-in, but we didn't go that far. She stopped and opened the door on the right and said. "This is the bathroom and this is the bedroom." She said as she opened the door opposite, put her hand on my cheek and said just make yourself at home, then turned and headed back down the hall.

It was a small bedroom with a single bed. One of the doors in the room was a closet so I opened my bag and hung up some slacks and shirts. The other door opened up into the den, being nosey I had to check it out, there was built-in bookcases, a nice executive style desk, an over stuffed leather sofa and easy chair, and a wet bar. The Margaritas had really gone to my head so I decided to take a shower and go to bed. While in the shower I heard a tapping on the door then it opened.

"I brought you some towels and wanted to make sure you had everything you needed." Linda said as I watched her over the top of the five foot shower door.

She had her hair down and was wearing a baby doll nightgown with an almost sheer robe. She sat a couple of large fluffy towels on the sink and turned around to face me and said.

"Do you need anything else in there?" As she handed me a bottle of shampoo over the top of the shower door.

"No I think that will do it, thank you." I told her and was glad she couldn't see through the shower door because I suddenly found myself in an embarrassing situation. Her robe was open and the nightgown she was wearing didn't leave much to the imagination. I thought for a second she was hitting on me, but immediately dismissed the idea as being wishful thinking.

"Well, if you can think of anything, my room is upstairs at the end of the hall. Goodnight."

Wow, I thought, this is one beautiful woman and it doesn't make any difference what she is wearing. I finished my shower and decided to go ahead and shave, then went to bed. I don't know how long I was asleep, but I was awaken by the smell of Jasmine and could see Linda's silhouette in the partially open doorway.

"Are you awake? I'm so restless I can't get to sleep, I think I had too much to drink. Do you mind?" She didn't give me a chance to answer, she just shut the door behind her and came over and sat on the side of the bed.

She kept talking, but I wasn't listening to her, my mind was on her hand rubbing my chest, and of course it wasn't long before I found myself in my previous embarrassing situation and it didn't take long before she discovered it for herself. She finally stopped talking stood up and said.

"Do you want me to leave, I really shouldn't be here, a married woman and all?"

I don't think I even answered her, but in the

soft moonlight coming through the window, I saw her drop the robe she was wearing and slip out of her nightgown. She then pulled back the covers and straddled me in the single bed like a jockey at the racetrack. After the third race she bent forward, kissed me softly on the cheek and whispered the strangest thing. She said, "thank you", that's all just "thank you", like *she* had something to thank *me* for. I'll never forget those words, she sounded so sincere. She got out of bed, put her robe on and picked up her nightgown and left the room.

The next morning I was awakened by the twins barging into the room and jumping on the bed. Little Mary was standing in the door way and said.

"Carla says you have to get up or you will be late for breakfast, and Carla likes for everyone to be prompt for meals."

"OK kids, I'm awake."

"Ask him Dino, ask him." Dannie, the little girl asked of her twin brother.

"Ask me what?"

"Mary said you took us to the zoo the last time you were here. Are you going to take us again?"

"I don't know kids, we'll see. Come on now, I have to get dressed."

Mary took the twins and went scurrying back down the hall. I sat on the edge of the bed for a moment with a slight hangover and wondered if last night had all been a dream, but the smell of Jasmine that permeated the bed linen told a different story. When I made it to the kitchen the kids were at the table and I don't know if they are waiting for me or Linda who is on the phone. When she hung up and sat down with us Carla served the twins oatmeal and scrambled eggs, toast and fried apples for the rest of us.

"That was Aimee on the phone, she squealed when I told her you were here. She will be arriving at 3pm, you can pick her up if you like."

"Yeah that will be great."

"What about the zoo, I want Mister Ron to take us to the zoo." Dino started a mini protest with his twin sister joining in, but it was quickly squashed by Carla.

"No zoo today, you two have swimming lessons and Mary has her tennis coach coming over. Maybe Aimee and Ron will take you to the zoo tomorrow."

After breakfast Linda got me a pair of the Judge's trunks and told me to join the family in the back by the swimming pool. The swimming trunks were a little large but they had a draw string. Since I had been in Europe for three years I appeared an odd sight with my pale body so I grabbed one of my short sleeve shirts and put it on without buttoning it. The kitchen door opened on to a small deck leading down to the swimming pool, at the opposite end was a combination pump and pool house where there was a group of women setting and several kids in the pool. On the left hand side of the pool area was a fenced off tennis court where Mary was having a lesson. Linda introduced me to Kim Jung, Silvie Greenburg and Karen Macklin. Silvie Greenburg patted me on the butt when I walked in front of her to set down and said. "He's cute Linda, where have you been hiding him?" Everyone had a laugh at my expense, but it was harmless. So I sat by the pool drinking Bloody Mary's with the women while all the kids played in the pool waiting on the swimming instructor. From what I got of the conversation it was actually Kim's turn to host the swimming class but her pool is being retiled.

After a lunch of melon balls and the swimming class almost over I excused myself to go get dressed to pick Aimee up. When I was ready to leave Linda came in to give me the flight number and directions to the airport. Linda made no indication that she wanted to talk about the night before so I didn't bring the subject up.

I spent two more nights at the house with no repeats of the first night. Aimee and I did take the kids to the zoo the next day. With me going to Vietnam, Aimee and I came to an understanding that it was OK to write, but she should not wait for me. I think it hurt her feelings a little at first, but since I was planning on making a career out of the Army, she realized it would be an impossible relationship so we decided to just be friends. So on the third day I said good-bye to the kids, Aimee and Carla and thanked Linda for a wonderful stay and she made me promise to come back if I got a chance.

CHAPTER 19.

The Choice

I drove back to Los Angeles then out to El Monte in the San Gabriel Valley to stay with my Uncle O'Dell and Bonnie. Between family dinners with my cousins, O'Dell, Bonnie and I hit all the local race-tracks, Santa Anita, Hollywood Park and Los Alamitos. I should have listened more to Bonnie than O'Dell, she had a system. "Bet the first gray of the day." "Always bet number 3 in the third race." and "You'll never be blue if you bet the Schu." As in Schumacher. Bonnie always did better than O'Dell and me even with all of our handicapping. We even got a trip in to Las Vegas and soon it was time to head north.

I flew up to San Francisco, changed into a uniform at the airport then caught a bus to the Oakland Army Terminal. I reported in a day early.

"Your orders are for Specialist Five Whitley. What's up with the Staff Sergeant stripes?" The civilian processing clerk asked me.

"Just a second." I said as I opened my bag and looked for the envelope with my promotion orders in it to give to him. "Here you go."

"Department of the Army. Is that where you're coming from Sergeant?"

"No, I'm coming from Germany."

"From Germany and going to Vietnam without a stateside assignment?"

"That's right."

"Wow, you must be something special Sergeant. Well, we'll be sure and treat you real special while you're here." The civilian clerk said sarcastically then continued. "I'll keep a copy of your orders and you can hump your bags over to building three and get in that *special* line, you'll recognize it, it's the one with everybody else in it."

What a smart ass I thought as I carried my suitcase and my duffle bag over to the correct building and got into the long line. When I finally got to the front, the Air Force Sergeant told me I was in Group 107-68 and to check in to barracks 21 and my processing would start tomorrow. There was a Spec Five in charge of the barracks, he logged me on his roster, told me he didn't have any NCO rooms left and to pick an empty bunk. I picked an upper close to the front then drew some sheets and a blanket.

Since I checked in a day early about half the group had started processing today. The half that arrived with me today would catch up without any problems, because it was one of those *hurry up and wait* deals. That night in the barracks after dinner. A lot of the guys were gathered around a couple of the NCOs who were going back to Vietnam for second tours. I listened from my bunk, some of the stuff they were saying was interesting, but I figured ninety percent of it was barracks bullshit, but it sure had some of the young kids scared shitless. There was a lot of kids who had been in the army only about four months, just enough time to go through basic training and in most cases infantry school, most of them were draftees but not all. It was a real mix of America from surfer boys to kids from the big cities, high school jocks to plow boys right of the farm, the only thing they had in common was they were all soldiers and some of them would not be coming home.

The next morning after breakfast we went for medical processing, got shots, then caught up with the rest of the group at lunch. The afternoon was personnel records processing to make sure all our records were up to date, next of kin, who to notify in case of an *emergency,* and life insurance, that short of thing. While there I was called out of the line and was in and lead in to a room with two guys in suits who identified themselves as FBI Agents.

"Sergeant Whitley, I'm Special Agent Cole and this is Special Agent LaPaglia. Why don't you have a seat. Do you want anything, a Coke or some coffee?"

"Yeah sure, I'll take some coffee. You want to tell me what this is all about?"

"We'll get to that in a minute. Frank you want to see if you can find us some coffee, black for me, and ah." Cole paused.

"Just cream in mine." I said as Agent LaPaglia left the room.

"While Frank is out of the room, I want to let you know that I know who you are and who you work for, so when he gets back just listen to him. He's going to make you an offer that could be beneficial to all of us."

I didn't know what this was all about, but I did know enough to keep my mouth shut until I found out. LaPaglia came back with some coffee and sat it down on the table, then he sat down and said.

"You comfortable now, you got everything you

need?" LaPaglia asked.

"What is this? Are you guys here to arrest me for something or what?"

"Why? Have you done something to be arrested for? Why don't you tell us about it. We're on your side, you know." Cole said then LaPaglia chimed in.

"Yeah, tell us about it. We can help you out, maybe make a deal or something. You know, scratch our back and we'll scratch yours."

"Look, I don't know what you guys are talking about, I don't know what you want and I'm not sure you have the right person."

"Oh, we have the right person, Ronald Whitley born in Louisville Kentucky, been in the army four and a half years, just back from Germany on your way to Vietnam. Sound like anybody you know?" Cole again.

"Yeah, that's me. Shouldn't I have a lawyer in here if you guys are accusing me of something?"

"You don't need a lawyer and we are not accusing you of anything. We want you to come and work for us." LaPaglia said.

"You mean you want me to join the FBI?"

"Not exactly, more of a trade off, you give us information and we pay you for it." LaPaglia continued. "It's called being a paid confidential informant."

"Look, in case you guys haven't figured it out yet, I have a job, I'm in the army."

"Let's cut the crap Whitley, I told you we already know who you are and who you really work for." Cole said getting irritated.

"OK, I give up. Who do I really work for?"

"You want to play games. I'll lay it out for you. We already had a file on you and when the Central Intelligence Agency put a block and classification of, not releasable to foreign agencies on your fingerprints, we made a request for your military records. They say you did a year and a half with the 3d Armored Division, but before that they say you spent a year and a half unassigned. Nobody spends eighteen months unassigned. So you tell us. What were you doing for those eighteen months."

"I'm sorry. I am not at liberty to discuss that information."

"We can read between the lines. This isn't our first day on the job. You are a hitter for the Agency. You work for them, we want you to work for us. Now do we know what you do or not?"

"Work for you, doing what, killing people?"

"No. The FBI doesn't work like that. We want you to be a confidential informant, like we told you." LaPaglia said.

"Well, even if what you are saying is true, which it's not, I'm shipping out for Vietnam tomorrow, and I don't know who I'd inform on anyway."

"That's just it, you don't have to go to Vietnam. We can get you discharged. We'll pay you the same money you are making now. All we want you to do is to move to Long Beach, look up your Uncle Paul. Stay close with the family and see if you can work your way in to the *business*."

"How are you going to get me discharged, you guys don't have that kind of pull."

"That's the easy part." Cole said then continued. "We furnish a dummy criminal history to the army, and they give you a Bad Conduct discharge."

"Let me see if I have this right. You're going to give me a criminal record, get me kicked out of the army, and you want me to spy on one of my step dad's brothers, that I only met one time when I was a kid. Then if I do give you the kind of information you want, you'll want me to testify in court and when it's all over you dump me and at best, I spend the rest of my life looking over my shoulder, and at worst I get killed by some Guido, no offense there Agent LaPaglia. Is that about it?"

"Except for the part that the government will protect you, relocate you when it's all over. Not to mention you'll be doing something for your country. You are patriotic you want to serve your country, or you wouldn't be in the army. Right?" Cole doing his *One for the Gipper* speech.

"You're right Agent Cole. That's why I'm in the army and if you don't mind, I think I'll take my chances in Vietnam."

"You know we could just release those fingerprints of yours, then wait till you need us." LaPaglia said then continued. "Then you'll be the one asking us for help. What do you think about that?"

"If I am what you think I am, not saying I am, but if I was and I reported what you just threatened me with and then you carried it out. What do you think your career would be worth?"

"Let's get out of here, we're wasting our time." Cole said as he stood up.

"Look Whitley, if you get to Vietnam and want to change your mind. Contact me and we'll work something out for you." LaPaglia said as he pushed one of his cards toward me then got up and left the room with Cole.

"I can't stand those *company* guys." I heard Cole say through the room partition as they left. Boy did those guys have a wrong number, I can't believe they think I work for the Central Intelligence Agency. I got into one mess just because I looked like someone, so I'm certainly not going to volunteer for another one.

After they left the area a Spec Four came into the room and told me I could join my group at building 18, uniform processing.

I had wasted my time packing the clothes I did. We empted everything out of our duffle bags except underwear and boxed everything up to be shipped home or put in storage. We were issued four sets of jungle fatigues, two pair of jungle boots and an assortment of underwear and socks. I kept a couple of Class A tan uniforms and some personal junk, boxed everything else up to be put in storage. After the sewing station for name tags we were finished for the day and told we would be leaving at 0900 hours, now that is *hurry up and wait* talk for we probably have a flight time of 1600 hours.

It was a long flight with a refueling stop in Guam, but we finally landed in Vietnam. It was a rude awakening as we walked down the ramp from the plane. The heat and humidity was over-whelming and the stink was almost unbearable. We were all herded to a processing area given temporary barracks assignments and told we would be proceeding to our units sometime tomorrow. Early the next morning I heard my name announced on the loudspeaker, telling me to bring my bags and report to the assembly area. I was met by a couple of Military Intelligence guys, one of them in jungle fatigues with just U.S. on his collars instead of rank, and the other one wearing a Hawaiian style aloha shirt.

"Are you Sergeant Whitley?" The one in the aloha shirt asked.

"That's me."

"You are going to be working for us in the field unit, but we have orders to run you by the Embassy in Saigon first." The guy in uniform said.

These guys didn't talk much on the way, except about fifteen minutes into the trip the one in uniform asked. "Ever been to Saigon before?"

"No. This is my first time in Vietnam."

"Don't worry, you'll love it. Saigon is the Paris of the Orient." The one in the aloha said and the one in uniform started laughing.

When we arrived at the Embassy, I was taken to a small office and told to go on in and they would wait for me outside. I went into the office and was unpleasantly surprised to hear a voice from my past. It was Jack Roark.

"Welcome to Vietnam, Viking."

In Conclusion

Yes, it was Jack Roark. Known to his mother as Little Jack, and by other people by other names, but more formally as John Fallon Roark, a man that I would learn to hate then grow to admire in some strange perverse way. I knew then that he was not done with me, and Viking would be called upon again, but those stories are for another time.

In 1967 several NATO military officers from four different countries were arrested on drug trafficking charges. Six of the officers were American. Three were allowed to resign from the military and three were reassigned out of Europe. No Turkish Diplomats were ever arrested or charged, but two were recalled to Turkey. Colonel Valerie Valerian, of the KGB, died at his home in Murmansk of an unknown illness shortly after arriving.

The only person ever charged in the death of the men in the warehouse, was Balzac the Bulgarian, and he served eight years in a French prison for conspiracy and activities against the best interest of France. The fate of Captain Martin is unknown to me, but Günter Schmitt would later become the Chief Security Officer for the German Ambassador to the United Nations.

ISBN 1425135773

9 781425 135775